I0831332

THE UNCANNY HOUSE

THE UNCANNY HOUSE

MARY L. PENDERED

Edited and with an introduction by
Gina R. Collia

Published by Nezu Press
Queensgate House,
48 Queen Street,
Exeter, Devon,
EX4 3SR,
United Kingdom.

This edition published 2024

The Uncanny House first published by Hutchinson & Co. Ltd., 1927.

ISBN-13: 978-1-917113-01-4

In the interest of preservation, the punctuation and spelling of the original first edition text have been maintained, and the original formatting has been used wherever possible. Only minor publisher errors and spelling inconsistencies have been silently corrected.

Yours truly
Mary L. Pendered.

Above: From *The Idler*, 1894.

Below: From a letter dated 1937, collection of Gina R. Collia.

Mary L. Pendered

Author, Suffragist, Pacifist, and Thoroughly Good Woman

by Gina R. Collia

Mary Lucy Pendered was born on 9 October 1858 at 4 Trafalgar Road (now Avenue), in the handsome, middle-class suburb of Peckham, to Thomas Pendered (1834-1906) and his wife, Elizabeth (née Hill, 1829-1885),[1] who had married the previous year.[2] Mary was the eldest of four children; John was born on 1 July 1861, Ellen Sophia followed on 2 June 1862, and William Hill arrived on 15 May 1863,[3] by which time the family had moved to 9 Gloucester Cottages, Park Road (now Parkfield Road).[4]

Elizabeth Pendered was the daughter of William Hill (1789-1870) and his wife, Mary (née Elliot c. 1798-1832).[5] William, one of the most important organ-builders in the country, was one half of Elliot and Hill of Tottenham Court Road, the other half being his father-in-law, Thomas Elliot (1758-1832), from whom he inherited the firm in 1832.[6] The two men built a number of famous organs; Thomas Elliot constructed a 'new magnificent organ' over the altar of Westminster Abbey for the coronation of King George IV in 1821, and in the 1830s the firm of Elliot and Hill built organs at York Minster, Ely Cathedral, King's College Chapel, and the newly-built Town Hall in Birmingham.[7]

Thomas Pendered, who was working as a merchant's clerk and living in London at the time of his marriage to Elizabeth, was born in Wellingborough, Northamptonshire.[8] His father, Joseph Pendered (1799-1872), started out as a cabinet, chair and sofa manufacturer in Northampton, offering 'good fashionable furniture, at a moderate price'.[9] In 1822, Joseph relocated his business to Market Square,

Wellingborough, where he operated as an 'Auctioneer, Upholsterer, and Paper Hanger'.[10] In 1854, he went into partnership with his eldest son, William, and Pendered & Son added 'Estate Agent' and 'Pianoforte Dealer' to its list of services.[11] By the early 1860s, William had taken on sole management of the furniture manufacturing side of the business, while his father acted as auctioneer, valuer and estate agent, and in April 1865, with the aim of giving each area 'undivided attention', the partnership was dissolved and the firm was split in two.[12] William, under the name of W. Pendered & Co., continued as a cabinet maker, upholsterer, and pianoforte dealer. Joseph Pendered went into partnership with his second son, Thomas, who by then had moved back to Wellingborough with his family; they formed J. Pendered & Son, 'Auctioneers, Valuers, Estate Agents, and Accountants'.[13]

When Mary's family first moved to Wellingborough from London, they lived at 38 Cambridge Street.[14] By 1881, they had moved to 'Redwell', Hatton Park, which remained in the Pendered family's possession for the next hundred years.[15] Mary was educated in Wellingborough, attended university extension courses, and studied for the Higher Local Examination, 'of which she passed one group (English Language and Literature)'.[16] Mary's family was a musical one, and she began her career as a vocalist. She studied for three years with a view to the light opera stage, receiving many offers of engagements,[17] but her passion for the stage was 'firmly discountenanced' by her family.[18]

Her family did not, however, object to her performing at various social and charitable events. She composed her own songs, and she regularly received encores and loud applause.[19] She was a favourite at the Temperance Choral Society's concerts, and she performed at and organised musical entertainments laid on at the dahlia flower shows which took place in Wellingborough.[20] For many years she organised an annual *café chantant* in aid of the Amalgamated Society of Railway Servants' Orphan Fund;[21] this particular entertainment had been Mary's idea, and the society's committee left everything in her hands, satisfied that she would always do her best. As a result, each year the event was more and more successful.

Mary first appeared in print as an author in 1886, at the age of twenty-seven. Her first published story, 'Chobertstein', appeared in the *Magazine of Music* in the August of that year, for which she received a cheque for two and a half guineas.[22] The same magazine published 'That Haunting Minor Strain' (1886), 'A Baneful Banjo' (1888), some poems and a short piece on 'Amateur Singing' (1887). In July 1889, her short story 'His Model' appeared in *Belgravia*.[23] In December 1890, 'Attraction!: A Melody in Two Keys' was published in the *Girl's Own Paper*, and the following year 'In Cowslip Time' appeared in the same periodical.

Mary's parents don't appear to have objected to her trying her hand at writing, but when she expressed a desire to move to London to become a journalist they were very much opposed to her doing so. They decreed that, should she choose to pursue such a career, she would have to 'earn her bed and board without financial assistance from home.'[24] Nonetheless, during the first half of 1892, she went ahead with her move to London,[25] took up residence in a single room in Kensington, and for a year 'battled for a place in the literary scheme of things', against her family's wishes and 'undaunted by the starvation wage of £1 a week.'[26] Her first employment was with a society weekly called *Life*, where she wrote a column called 'Twitters, by Tom Tit'; she 'attended weddings, described trousseaux, canvassed for advertisements, corrected proofs, harried the printers, corresponded with all and sundry for the paper, was art critic,' and did 'everything except sweep out the office.'[27] From there, she went on to work as sub-editor for the London edition of the *Detroit Free Press*, where she met Hall Caine and George Bernard Shaw and became 'well known to the denizens of Bohemia'.[28] According to the *Aberdeen Evening Express*, at the age of thirty-five she was 'tall and stately, brown-haired, blue-eyed, of the proverbial English type', and she could 'handle a racquet and a pair of reins better than most women.'[29]

Mary's short story 'Mademoiselle Guarier' appeared in *Christmas Arrows*, the *Quiver* Christmas annual for 1892, and 'A Swerve Aside' was published in the *Quiver* in May 1893. A few weeks later, Griffith, Farran and Co. published her first novel, *Dust and Laurels: A Study in Nineteenth Century Womanhood*, the story of modern woman Vera Grace and her various romantic entanglements. It was dedicated 'to that hybrid complication, the woman of to-day, whose food is fruit of the tree of knowledge of good and evil, and whose drink is the intoxicating ether of freedom and independence'. Described by the *Aberdeen Evening Express* as 'one of the most adventurous books of the season',[30] nearly every English reviewer flattered the author and abused her heroine.[31] 'Despite the undoubted ability of the authoress,' wrote the reviewer for the *Gentlewoman*, 'the heroine of "Dust and Laurels" is distinctly vulgar, which is worse than being "frightfully thrilling".'[32] According to the reviewer for *The Bookseller*, if Vera really was a type of nineteenth-century woman it would be 'so much the worse for the century'.[33] *Black & White* found her 'detestable', and the *Daily Telegraph & Courier* found the novel 'clever but disagreeable'.[34] The lesson to be learned from reading about Vera's entanglements, according to the critic for the *Manchester Chronicle*, was 'that a woman ought to marry young, otherwise she becomes incapable of her mission on earth.'[35]

When *Dust and Laurels* came out, Mary was still doing what she called 'literary hack work'.[36] A year later, after completing her novel *A Pastoral Played Out*, and having 'made her mark as a novelist of power', Mary gave up journalism and returned to her family home.[37] Much later in life, at the age of seventy-five, she confessed that she hadn't liked working as a journalist.[38] Newspaper hack work involved working at 'top speed' to meet deadlines, without time for revision, and it was a marvel to her that any journalist could turn in well-written 'copy' in the short time available.[39] 'I need time to think about what I write,' she explained, 'and I like to revise my work.'[40] At the beginning of her career, the creative part of her work was done at night because she found 'the imaginative faculties are more active and less illusive.' Revision was done in the mornings, when the 'critical and practical side of the mind is most alert and assertive.'[41]

Mary began contributing to Jerome K. Jerome's *Idler* in 1894, when, within The Idler's Club column, she was one of an all-female group of respondents to the question of 'How to Court the Advanced Woman'.[42] Under the heading 'Deferential Domination Required', she suggested that the advanced woman—the new, independent woman as opposed to the 'traditional' one—'does not so much require to be courted as convinced'. The new woman, she explained, would be quite willing to marry if her suitor could 'command her respect, attract her senses, and assure her of his right to her'; she was to be wooed by means of 'a kind of deferential domination, a peremptory homage', by a man whose character 'does not wither under her criticism'.

In 1897, within the same column and on the subject of 'Early Marriages', Mary wrote that it was a very good thing for a man to marry early, as he was 'sure to fall into bad habits' if he failed to do so.[43] But women, she suggested, needed to be 'out' long enough—well into their twenties—to discover who they were. As a result, she supported 'compulsory marriage for men before the age of twenty-five and prohibition of it for women under that age'. She admitted that the former group may feel hard done to, as many women 'lose their charm with their teens', and most men prefer charm to all other things, but she pointed out 'what a good time girls would have before the prime business of life had to be considered!' Early marriage for women, she concluded, could not be abolished entirely without the total abolition of man, and she was not prepared to advocate that… 'at present.'

During the next few years, a number of Mary's short stories were published in various periodicals, including the *Idler*, *New Century Review*, *Longman's Magazine*, *Belgravia*, and *Cassell's Family Magazine. To Luniland with a Moon Goblin*, an illustrated fairytale for children, was published in 1897, and Mary's third novel, *An Englishmen*, a tale of class distinction in which the hero is a handsome middle-class tradesman, followed in 1899.[44] *An Englishman* received positive reviews, and William Leonard Courtney thought it to be one of the best books of 1899; he described it as 'a thoroughly wholesome, sympathetic, effective story…handled with considerable adroitness and manifesting no inconsiderable originality of characterisation'.[45] The book sold very well and a new edition was issued by Mills & Boon in 1912.

The Truth about Man by 'A Spinster' was published by Hutchinson and Co., in 1905.[46] It was written as a witty response to T. W. H. Crossland's *Lovely Woman*, in which he insulted women, claiming that only kings and coal porters kept their wives in their proper place; to 'bring the enemy to whatever small sense she possesses', he recommended that ladies should make fewer appearances in public places, have less freedom, and receive fewer compliments.[47] In *The Truth about Man*, Mary claimed that wives are generally content with Man 'as a husband and breadwinner', whereas the variety of spinster who regards marriage as a snare—who avoids it 'while she sports round the rim of it'—has more time and opportunity and is best placed to probe Man as 'a problem', which is what she, as the type of spinster described, then proceeded to do. She based her analysis upon personal experience, having 'been loved by three Americans, two Frenchmen, one German, one Irishman, one Swiss, three Scotsmen, and two or three Colonials'. She did not, she explained, intend her remarks as an attack; no indeed, for 'dear Man himself' is 'certainly most estimable and delightful—till you know him!'

Woman, she argued, was learning from experience that it was perfectly possible to be happy without being married. Marriage was a lottery, and, while there were prizes to be had, women embarked upon the career of a wife knowing that they stood a good chance of experiencing suffering 'and even death'.

> 'Give a woman certain interests in life, something to love and to be absorbed in; insure her a safe income, good friends, enough amusement and variety to spice existence, and see whether she cannot have a real good time without a husband.'

The Truth about Man sold very well indeed and was widely reviewed.[48] The *Review of Reviews* called it 'both amusing and provocative';[49] 'it puts pepper in the eyes and it wakes one up'.[50] The *Northampton Herald* thought it a 'seriously amusing shillingsworth'.[51] 'Her standpoint is distinctly original,' wrote the reviewer for *The Era*, 'and the results are exquisitely piquant'.[52] The *Yorkshire Post*, on the other hand, 'soundly trounced it, spreading themselves in a scathing review', and called Mary 'a minx', which very much amused her.[53]

At some time during 1907, Mary moved to The Fold, Beltinge, in Herne Bay, Kent. In December 1907, when the Railway Servants' Orphan Fund held its annual fundraiser in Wellingborough, the *café chantant* took place without Mary's presence for the first time in seventeen years.[54] Though unable to be present, she continued to write to the *Wellingborough News*, urging support for the fund, in which she still held 'the deepest interest'.[55]

Mary was 'much charmed by the air and surroundings of Beltinge' and advised several of her friends to take houses in the area.[56] She was not, however, much charmed by her neighbours' 'obnoxious and destructive' poultry. In a letter of complaint to the Blean Rural District Council, that was published in the *Herne Bay Press* on 18 January 1908, she complained that her neighbours, for the sake of a few cheap eggs, let their 'irrepressible poultry' run wild in other people's gardens, including her own, scratching up and destroying peas, beans and cabbages.[57]

In June 1908, Mary wrote a long letter to the editor of the *Wellingborough News* on the subject of women's suffrage.[58] The paper printed her letter, which included extracts from a speech made by Israel Zangwill the previous year, but its 'printing wags' included a number of errors that left her open to looking foolish as a woman and less than competent as a writer. In her follow-up letter, she corrected the errors and added:

> 'I have long had the presumption to believe myself capable of using a vote usefully, [at] least as capable as many of the male voters who nightly roll home from their pubs to their long-suffering wives. And I don't believe a vote

would hurt me a bit. If I left my home once in three years to inscribe a cross upon a card at a polling station, I feel sure it would not unsex me in the least, nor rub the bloom off either my modesty or my domestic virtues.'[59]

In February 1909, Mary wrote a letter to the editor of the *Herne Bay Press* on the subject of the newly-formed Women's National Anti-Suffrage League. Was there not, she asked, something extremely ignoble, even cruel, about the actions of women who, on the basis that they were happy with their lot, fought tooth and nail to deprive other women, unhappy with theirs, of the right to improve their condition. The 'so-called sex war', she suggested, threatened to become a war of woman v. woman rather than man v. woman, of 'the idle and happy women v. the hard-working and unhappy'.[60] She urged sympathisers to aid in halting the spread of 'ignorance and uncharity' and suggested that there did not exist 'a single "Anti" earnest enough to go to prison for her faith'.[61] Her letter received a response from Edith Somervell,[62] Honorary Secretary of the Anti-Suffrage League, who explained that women's suffrage—which 'would inevitably increase largely the ignorant vote'—had never been tried in a country which could 'be compared with Imperial Britain' and posed a 'profound danger to the Empire and the race'.[63] Mary's response was to point out the fact that 'Anti' arguments were 'practically the same as those brought forward by Southern Americans in defence of slavery', by people 'afraid of a leap in the dark' and 'satisfied with things as they ought *not* to have been.'[64]

In 1912 and 1913, Mary produced what *The Bookman* called 'her three most characteristic novels of country life in Northamptonshire': *At Lavender Cottage*, *Phyllida Flouts Me*, and *Lily Magic*.[65] Whilst some of Mary's earlier work had attracted criticism for being 'immoral and too daring', these three novels received praise for being wholesome and pretty.[66] Reviewers described *At Lavender Cottage* as a 'fresh, sweet, natural book',[67] thought *Phyllida Flouts Me* 'an uncommonly pretty story',[68] and found *Lily Magic* 'wholesomely fresh and stimulating'.[69]

Mary 'ever declined to write in a groove'.[70] On the subject of the variety in her work, she said:

> 'I cannot and don't want to write two books alike. I cannot make a name for a certain type of book, because my fancy pulls in so many directions. At one moment I long to write, like Herrick, "of books, of blossoms, birds and flowers, of April, May, of June and July flowers." At another time I feel impelled to write of poor, frail, fallen humankind. At another I write of naughty people and their passions. Or again I have a sudden desire to recreate a once living man or woman in biography. Or I feel sententious and wish to spend myself in essays. Or a dramatic inspiration seizes me and I turn to write a play.'[71]

Mary had begun attending, and speaking at, suffragist meetings in Herne Bay in 1909;[72] by the following year, she was presiding over them.[73] In June 1913, 'law-abiding suffragists' held an open-air meeting, 'of a most orderly description', at the top of Beacon Hill, on Herne Bay Downs, and, despite the fact that a cold, north-westerly wind was blowing, a considerable crowd gathered to hear the speeches.[74] Further open-air meetings took place the following month, and by August the ranks of the Herne Bay society had swollen enough for it to become affiliated with the National Union of Women's Suffrage Societies. In October, a committee, president, treasurer, secretary, and chairman were elected, and by the middle of November a social evening was organised, at which the membership rose from thirty-five to forty-nine.[75] The society was renamed The Herne Bay Society for Women's Suffrage, and Mary, the society's president, took on the role of press secretary.[76]

At the outbreak of war in 1914, the Herne Bay suffragists ceased political activity and devoted themselves to war work, with the understanding that their fight for the vote would resume 'with doubly increased vigour' at the cessation of hostilities.[77] Mary registered as a voluntary worker, and she and her sister Ellen instigated the opening of The Soldiers' Club at Mr Mitchell's garage, Beltinge, for 'music, reading and writing', for which a call was immediately sent out for donations of magazines, writing paper, pens, pencils, and 'anyone able to play and sing'.[78] In 1915, the club moved to a large bungalow, which had been lent for the purpose, and wounded soldiers from the Military Hospital found it 'very cosy and homelike'; Mary became chairman of the committee and entertainment organiser, and she took on 'her fair share in the general housework and canteen management.'[79]

A number of years later, at the beginning of the Second World War, Mary wrote of her experiences during the First World War. She was present for the first air raid warning that went out over Herne Bay; it turned out to be the last. It went off at about 11:30 at night, when the first Zeppelin came over, and the whole town turned out into the streets to watch the skies. Mary was in bed and got up to find all of her neighbours in the road. The police could not cope with the crowds, and the warnings were discontinued.[80] The 'continued and violent practising of the big guns' at Sheerness 'made writing a misery to her', and she found the noise so intolerable that eventually, in order to complete the novel she was working on, she was forced to leave her seaside home.[81]

In the spring of 1917, Mary resigned from her position as president of The Herne Bay Society for Women's Suffrage, left Beltinge, and returned to her family's home in Northamptonshire, where she lived with her widowed brother, John, and took on the role of president of the Wellingborough branch of the National Union of Women's Suffrage Societies.[82] Of Mary and her home, Redwell, H. E. Bates wrote:

> 'Wellingborough is to be congratulated in having so charming a novelist as Miss Mary L. Pendered in its midst. One wonders if any of her charm is due to environment, for she lives in a beautiful house, set in gardens that Rupert Brooke would have loved for their beauty and colour and scent. One hardly knows whom to envy most—Miss Pendered or Wellingborough.'[83]

Throughout the war years, Mary continued to write. Chapman and Hall published *Plain Jill* in 1915, followed by *The Secret Sympathy* in 1916, and in the same year J. M. Dent published *The Book of Common Joys*. The latter is a collection of essays, skilfully woven together to form 'a series of reflections which alike soothe and stimulate', 'Written in Autumn Sunshine for those who have left Summer behind', on the simple joys of being alive, reading, country life, gardens, etc.[84] Mary loved the countryside and was a keen gardener, and, though she did not like complete isolation from human contact, she found that 'Silence and leisure are the sweetest things on earth'.[85] She loved 'the joy of morning, and the cool, calm peace of evening' and found both in her garden.[86]

Mary was an active, productive person throughout her life. She was also an extremely clever and amusing one; she had an excellent sense of humour, and she loved to laugh and to make other people laugh with her.

'For the sense of humour may we be truly thankful! It is the *sauce piquant* at the daily fare of life, and those who are blessed with it in the smallest degree may feel a deep compassion for those who lack it; though, fortunately for the latter, they are unaware of their deprivation.'[87]

On 11 November 1918, after more than four years of conflict and the horrendous loss of millions of lives, the First World War came to an end. A month earlier, the League of Nations Union, the most influential organisation in the British peace movement, was formed.[88] Its goal was to secure justice, peace and security for all nations based on the ideals of The League of Nations.[89] On 5 September 1920, under the auspices of the League of Nations Union, and under Mary's direction, a pageant and play entitled *The Crowning of Peace* was performed to a large audience at the Wellingborough Palace. Mary said that her reason for producing the pageant 'was her passionate burning zeal for the League of Nations'.[90] It was not only the thought of men lying in agony on the field of battle that moved her to action, for there were worse things than that; men who went to war were changed by the experience and 'had to become no longer human, but wild beasts, before they could do the sanguinary work they were called on to do.'[91] If only people would think about this, she explained, they would come to realise that 'anything to stop war should at least be tried'.[92]

Mary addressed meetings of 'co-operators' in Wellingborough and took every opportunity to voice her support for the League of Nations Union.[93] In April 1924, a *café chantant* took place for the benefit of Greek refugees, in league with the Wellingborough branch of the union, and Mary, its instigator, presided over what turned out to be a very successful event.[94] In November 1924, the Northamptonshire Council for the League of Nations Union was formed; the Bishop of Peterborough was elected as president, and Mary was chosen as one of its vice presidents.[95] She took a great deal of interest in local and national politics; she was a member of the Fabian Society for more than forty years and was present at the victory celebrations when W. G. Cove was re-elected as Labour MP for Wellingborough.[96] Mary cared about the wellbeing of those within and outside of her community, supported equality, and continued to call for peace until the day she died.

Peace was the subject of Mary's four-act play *The Quaker*, first performed in Rushden on 18 March 1926, where it received an enthusiastic reception. In the play, the hero, Nathanael Harlock, is involved in a duel, contrary to the faith in which he has been raised. On the point of victory over his opponent, he lays down his sword and refuses further combat. As she explained to her audience in Rushden, Mary had devoted her life to the cause of peace, and she wrote the play with a distinct purpose: 'to instil a dislike for war', and to force home the principles of which she was so stalwart a supporter.[97] The proceeds from performances of the play were divided between the League of Nations Union and a local cause.[98] *The Quaker* was put on at various locations during the next few years; it was performed at the Royalty in London in November 1930.[99]

The Uncanny House was published by Hutchinson & Co. Ltd. in 1927. It is the story of Peggy and Percy Dacre who, having bought The Beeches—commonly referred to as 'Hell Corner' by the locals—for an absurdly cheap price, move into their new home with their four young children only to discover that it is haunted. The previous owner, old Mr Barker, was a curmudgeon who underfed his dogs to make them vicious and kept his low-paid staff loyal with promises of legacies that never materialised. But, though its owner acquired something of a reputation, the house itself, a villa located on the outskirts of a country town, is an ordinary sort of place; the only unusual thing about it is its lack of electricity. Peggy describes it as 'about as commonplace as they make 'em.'[100]

> 'It was all nonsense, she told herself, about the house being haunted. It was a nice, homely, commonplace sort of house; not a bit the kind in which any ghost would disport itself. Like most of us, she visualized the haunted house as of the Moated Grange type—a place where awful crimes had been committed.'[101]

When strange things begin to happen in the Dacres' perfectly normal home, Percy, a firm unbeliever when it comes to all things ghostly, goes to great lengths to explain the unexplainable. Peggy, on the other hand, is 'sensitive' and becomes increasingly frustrated by her husband's willingness to believe the ridiculous rather than give credence to anything supernatural; 'such a form of scepticism, dependent on believing absurdities, was beyond her ken.'[102]

In comparison with Mary's previous novels, *The Uncanny House* received relatively little attention from reviewers. The *Northern Whig* described it as 'a simple, unpretentious tale, the characters of which are all very natural, likeable people'.[103] 'Mary L. Pendered', wrote the *Dundee Courier*, 'gets the creepy atmosphere of a house in which strange things happen… the dramatic situations are well handled and the eerie feeling maintained'.[104] And the reviewer for *The Bookman* thought that 'those who like to indulge their eerie fancies and give their imagination a little exercise' would enjoy 'participating in the weird experiences' of Peggy and her sceptical, matter-of-fact husband.[105]

Mary had more than a passing interest in the paranormal. It is obvious from her characters' comments in *The Uncanny House* that she had read Frederic W. H. Myers' *Human Personality and its Survival of Bodily Death*, published in 1903, which presented an overview of his pioneering research into the unconscious mind, the nature of human personality, and the possibility of the continued existence of human consciousness after death of the physical body. Myers proposed a theory that explained ghost-seeing as the result of telepathy and the projection of a 'phantasm', whether on the part of a living person—a 'phantasm of the living'—or a dead one. On the subject of ghost stories, Mary wrote:

> 'Whether we believe in the tales or not, whether we are born sceptics or put some faith in psychic phenomena, there are few of us who cannot enjoy a ghost yarn round a Christmas fire. And at this period we have come to prefer the unexplained, the "authenticated" ghost story. Once it was the fashion to account for every occult experience by some absurd anti-climax; but it is not so to-day. We don't like our ghost to be explained away, though he may have a moral reason for his appearance.'[106]

The Forsaken House at Misty Vale was published in the autumn of 1932 by Heath Cranton. 'Written in that delightful style which is so peculiarly Miss Pendered's own', it tells the story of Celia Grey, a fifty-year-old, unmarried writer who, having longed for a home of her own for decades, thinks all her prayers have been answered when she inherits her uncle's house.[107] But Clew Lodge is a property with an uncanny reputation. It is a 'grim and daunting' place, desolate and derelict, having been 'left to the forces of corruption' since Uncle Jerrold abandoned it—because he 'could not stand the whispering'—a decade prior to his death. When Celia begins to hear those whispers too, she feels unable to go on sleeping in it alone; she has 'the horrors' when she tries. Like Peggy Dacre in

The Uncanny House, Celia doesn't have a lot of options when is comes to where she lives; she can't afford to give up her house. But unlike Peggy, Celia *wants* a matter-of-fact sceptic to scoff at her when she senses the presence of something supernatural. So, she invites plain, sensible, no-nonsense Miss Flack to live with her, whose scorn gives her 'a sense of security and support'. 'There is nothing gruesome or repellent' about the book, wrote the reviewer for the *Northampton Mercury*; though 'gripping it certainly is', and its author 'who knows well how to create atmosphere, sustains the suspense admirably'.[108] 'The strangeness of the forsaken house is convincing,' wrote another critic, 'but no one need be afraid to read it before turning off the light.'[109]

During the last years of Mary's life, she devoted only two hours of each day to her writing; 'I am on lots of committees in Wellingborough', she explained to a reporter for the *Northampton Mercury*, 'and I am running this big family here.'[110] She did not work in a study or at a table, preferring to sit in 'a big, deep armchair by the corner of the fireside, her feet on a stool and a board on her knee.'[111] She wrote quickly, as she always had, and thoroughly revised the first manuscript before typing up a second one and revising that. Unlike the early days of her career, she preferred to write during the morning, finding that, though she still considered herself a 'young thing',[112] she was tired in the evening and 'glad to get to bed.'[113] Her favourite authors were Charles Dickens—she was vice president of the Wellingborough branch of the Dickens Fellowship—and Sir Walter Scott; amongst modern writers, she liked Francis Brett Young.[114]

Some time between the autumn of 1935 and the spring of 1936, Mary moved to The Spinney, Great Addington, where she lived alone, with the help of her housekeeper, for the remainder of her life.[115] She remained active in every respect; she was an indefatigable writer and a tireless campaigner for peace and equality. She gave talks to, and produced plays for, the Overstone and Sywell branch of the Women's Institute, and she continued to pen letters to the local newspapers on a regular basis. And, still a practising vocalist and musician at the age of seventy-seven, after hearing all about 'the principles of pianoforte technique as expounded by that incomparable master, Tobias Matthay', she 'resolutely attempted to reorganise her considerable pianistic gifts upon entirely new lines'.[116]

In April 1939, though still recovering from influenza, Mary gave a talk at the Wellingborough Co-operative Old Folk's Party, at which she entertained six hundred or so elderly people. A report of the event appeared in the *Northamptonshire Evening Telegraph* under the headline 'Authoress Attacks the "Mike".'[117] At eighty years of age, she had so clear a voice that she had no need of a microphone, and she made that fact clear; 'Take away that bauble!' she declared, very much to the amusement of her audience. She then proceeded to recite a number of verses, declaring the whole thing 'a great lark'.

Mary was taken ill on 15 December 1940. She was transferred by ambulance to the home of her niece, Mary Stephens, and she died four days later. She was eighty-two years old.[118] Her funeral service, which was 'of simple character' in accordance with her wishes, was held in the old parish church of Great Addington on Monday 23 December.[119] There was no music; the rector, Rev. D. H. Meggy, read the hymn 'Now the Labourer's Task Is O'er' while the congregation stood in silence.[120] Following her cremation at Kettering Crematorium, her ashes were scattered in the consecrated portion of the Garden of Remembrance.[121]

In her will, Mary left all copies of her peace plays—*William Penn*, *The Quaker*, and *Banish the Bogie*—and all proceeds and royalties derived from them to the League of Nations Union. She left various bequests to good causes, including the Society of Authors, for its pension fund, Wellingborough Cottage Hospital, the juvenile branch of Wellingborough Labour Institute, and the Committee of Wellingborough Free Library. She left £50 each to her maid and housekeeper, and '£1,000 upon trust for her former companion, Marta Davies, for life'.[122]

Mary left behind at least three completed manuscripts, 'two novels and a pastoral', which remained unpublished following the outbreak of war in 1939. Two of her books were being translated into Danish at the time of her death, and she was eager to see how they would turn out. And she had also begun writing her memoirs, which, had they been completed and published, would have proved immensely interesting to those who knew her when she was alive and those who have discovered her work since her death.[123]

Mary L. Pendered, *Northampton Mercury*, 1933.

In his intimate tribute to his dear old friend, the author Reginald Underwood described his old friend as 'a fine personality… incapable of a mean word or action' and 'utterly honest'; 'There was in her make-up no taint of snobbery… She was, in short, an essentially and thoroughly good woman.[124] Though she was drawn to

Quakerism, Mary found the various religious beliefs and doctrines too limiting and 'maintained a tolerant agnosticism' throughout her life.[125]

> 'She has gone forth into the Great Unknown with her colours flying, bravely prepared to meet the all or the nothing that may be in store.'[126]

Notes

1 *London, England, Church of England Births and Baptisms, 1813-1923.* Peckham was in the parish of Camberwell, London.

2 *London, England, Church of England Marriages and Banns, 1754-1938.*

3 *London, England, Church of England Births and Baptisms, 1813-1923.*

4 Their home on Park Road in Peckham was a couple of miles or so from Trafalgar Road.

5 *London, England, Church of England Births and Baptisms, 1813-1923.*

6 12 Tottenham Court Road, London. *London, England, City Directories, 1736-1943*, 1840, p. 171.

7 *Morning Post*, 2 July 1821, p. 3.

8 Thomas Pendered was living on New Kent Road, Surrey (which now falls within the London borough of Southwark) at the time of his marriage. *1871 England Census* and *London, England, Church of England Births and Baptisms, 1813-1923.*

9 *Northampton Mercury*, 9 March 1822, p. 3.

10 Ibid., and 7 March 1835, p. 2. Wellingborough is a market town in the civil parish of North Northamptonshire.

11 *Northampton Mercury*, 2 September, 1854, p. 2, and 8 April 1865, p. 4.

12 *Northampton Mercury*, 8 April 1865, p. 4.

13 Ibid.

14 *1871 England Census.*

15 *1881 England Census* and *England & Wales, National Probate Calendar (Index of Wills and Administrations), 1858-1995.* Redwell remained in the family until the death of Richard Dudley Pendered, Mary's nephew (son of her brother John), in 1979.

16 *Morning Leader*, 31 July 1893, p. 3. Extension lectures prepared candidates for the Higher Local Examination. The examinations, open to female students over the age of eighteen, were designed to enable women to

demonstrate academic ability in order to apply to study at university.

17 *Morning Leader*, 31 July 1893, p. 3.

18 *Northampton Mercury*, 24 March 1933, p. 12.

19 *Northampton Mercury*, 15 December 1899, p. 7.

20 *Northampton Mercury*, 30 October 1889, p. 10, and 17 September 1897, p. 7.

21 *Café chantant:* Café concert. *Northampton Mercury*, 1 January 1904, p. 5.

22 *Morning Leader*, 31 July 1893, p. 3, and *Herne Bay Press*, 15 April 1911, p. 1.

23 Several poems by Mary were published in the *Magazine of Music*: 'I Love Thee So' (1886), 'The Lady is so Sweet' (1887), 'When Kissing is in Fashion' (1888), and 'A Little Bird Told Me' (1888).

24 *Northampton Mercury*, 24 August 1934, p. 6.

25 *Morning Leader*, 31 July 1893, p. 3.

26 *Northampton Mercury*, 24 August 1934, p. 6, and *Herne Bay Press*, 15 April 1911, p. 1.

27 Ibid.

28 *Northampton Mercury*, 24 August 1934, p. 6, and *Aberdeen Evening Express*, 15 July 1893, p. 2.

29 *Aberdeen Evening Express*, 15 July 1893, p. 2.

30 Ibid.

31 Note to the American edition, published D. Appleton and Company in 1894.

32 *Gentlewoman*, 5 August 1893, p. 20.

33 *The Bookseller*, 5 August 1893, p. 14.

34 *Black & White*, 15 July 1893, p. 20, and *Daily Telegraph & Courier*, 24 July 1893, p. 7.

35 *Manchester Courier*, 18 November 1893, p. 10.

36 *Northampton Mercury*, 24 March 1933, p. 12.

37 *Morning Leader*, 19 March 1894, p. 1. *A Pastoral Played Out*, originally intended as a three-volume novel, was completed in the spring of 1894 and published by Heinemann one year later.

38 *Northampton Mercury*, 24 August 1934, p. 6.

39 Ibid.

40 Ibid.

41 *Northampton Mercury*, 24 March 1933, p. 12.

42 *Idler*, vol. VI, August 1894 to January 1895, pp. 204-206.

43 *Idler*, vol. XII, August 1897 to January 1898, p. 425.

44 *To Luniland with a Moon Goblin* was published by Sanders, Bellamy and Sons of Wellingborough. The illustrations were provided by Dorothy Hope, a child of ten. *An Englishman* was published by Methuen and Co.

45 *The Bookman*, October 1919, p. 6.

46 Previously published by the *Lady's Realm* as a 'series of fearless and trenchant papers', beginning in the November 1904 issue.

47 *Morpeth Herald*, 20 June 1903, p. 7.

48 *Northampton Mercury*, 24 August 1934, p. 6.

49 *Review of Reviews*, August 1805, p. 204.

50 Ibid.

51 *Northampton Herald*, 11 October 1912, p. 13, in response to the publication of a new cheap edition.

52 *The Era*, 21 September 1912, p. 27.

53 *Northampton Mercury*, 24 August 1934, p. 6.

54 *Wellingborough News*, 3 January 1908, p. 6.

55 *Wellingborough News*, 25 December 1908, p. 5.

56 *Herne Bay Press*, 18 January 1908, p. 2.

57 Ibid.

58 *Wellingborough News*, 19 June 1908, p. 5.

59 *Wellingborough News*, 26 June 1908, p. 5.

60 *Herne Bay Press*, 20 February 1909, p. 6.

61 Ibid.

62 Wife of the composer Arthur Somervell and grandmother of the novelist Elizabeth Jane Howard.

63 *Herne Bay Press*, 6 March 1909, p. 6.

64 H*erne Bay Press*, 13 March 1909, p. 6.

65 Published by Mills & Boon. *The Bookman*, October 1919, p. 6.

66 Ibid.

67 *Bedfordshire Times and Independent*, 27 December 1912, p. 5.

68 *Dundee Courier*, 20 February 1913, p. 7.

69 *Northampton Mercury*, 17 October 1913, p. 5.

70 *The Bookman*, October 1919, p. 6.

71 Ibid.

72 *Votes for Women*, 5 November 1909, p. 93.

73 *Herne Bay Press*, 19 March 1910, p. 8.

74 *Herne Bay Press*, 28 June 1913, p. 1.

75 *Herne Bay Press*, 7 February 1914, p. 1.

76 Ibid.

77 *Herne Bay Press*, 13 November 1915, p. 1.

78 *The Bookman*, August 1916, p. 118, and *Herne Bay Press*, 21 November 1914, p. 8. Ellen Pendered, then Mrs Harley, was by then living at The Sheeling, Beltinge.

79 *Herne Bay Press*, 6 November 1915, p. 1, and *The Bookman*, August 1916, p. 118.

80 *Northamptonshire Evening Telegraph*, 12 December 1939, p. 6.

81 The Bookman, August 1916, p. 118.

82 *Herne Bay Press*, 1 December 1917, p. 1, and *The Common Cause*, 7 December 1917, p. 435.

83 Dean R. Baldwin, *H. E. Bates: A Literary Life*. Susquehanna University Press, 1987, p. 55.

84 *The Sphere*, 13 May 1916, p. 30.

85 *Northampton Mercury*, 24 August 1934, p. 6. She wrote, in *The Book of Common Joys*, 'my own ideal of the country does not figure complete solitude', that 'would not spell happiness for me' (p. 221).

86 *Northampton Mercury*, 24 August 1934, p. 6.

87 *The Book of Common Joys*, J. M. Dent, 1916, p. 189.

88 The League of Nations Union was formed by the merger of two older organisations: the League of Free Nations Association and the League

of Nations Society. The new union's first president was Viscount Grey (*Daily News*, 25 October 1918, p. 3).

89 The League of Nations, founded on 10 January 1920, was the first worldwide organisation dedicated to securing world peace and security via international cooperation.

90 *Midland Mail*, 10 September 1920, p. 2.

91 Ibid.

92 Ibid.

93 *Northampton Mercury*, 18 February 1921, p. 10.

94 *Northampton Chronicle and Echo*, 5 April 1924, p. 7.

95 *Peterborough Standard*, 28 November 1924, p. 10.

96 *Herne Bay Press*, 15 April 1911, p. 1, and *Northampton Chronicle and Echo*, 19 January 1925, p. 8.

97 *Northampton Mercury*, 26 March 1926, p. 5.

98 Ibid.

99 J. P. Wearing, *The London Stage 1930-1939: A Calendar of Productions, Performers, and Personnel.* Plymouth: Rowman & Littlefield, 2014, p. 66.

100 Nezu Press edition (2024), p. 3.

101 Ibid. p. 35.

102 Ibid. p. 92

103 *Northern Whig*, 22 October 1927, p. 9.

104 *Dundee Courier*, 29 November 1927, p. 5.

105 *The Bookman*, January 1928, p. 236.

106 Light, 28 December 1912, p. 618, quoting an article from the Daily Chronicle.

107 *Northampton Mercury*, 7 October 1932, p. 9.

108 Ibid.

109 *The Spectator*, 1 October 1932, p. 40.

110 *Northampton Mercury*, 24 August 1934, p. 6.

111 Ibid.

112 *Northampton Mercury*, 27 December 1940, p. 8.

113 *Northampton Mercury*, 24 August 1934, p. 6.

114 Ibid. She contributed may articles to *The Dickensian*, see vols 37-38, 1941, p. 163.

115 Mary moved to Great Addington, about seven or eight miles from Redwell, when she was seventy-seven years old, some time after 9 October 1935, see *Market Harborough Advertiser and Midland Mail*, 27 December 1940, p. 5. In April 1936, she placed an advertisement for a housekeeper in the *Peterborough Standard* (17 April 1936), by which time she was living in Great Addington. So, she moved some time between October 1935 and April 1936.

116 *Market Harborough Advertiser and Midland Mail*, 27 December 1940, p. 5.

117 *Northamptonshire Evening Telegraph*, 17 April 1939, p. 3.

118 *Northampton Mercury*, 20 December 1940, p. 10. Mary died at Beechwood, Overstone Park, the home of her niece Mary Stephens, née Mary Elizabeth Pendered, daughter of John Pendered.

119 *Market Harborough Advertiser and Midland Mail*, 27 December 1940, p. 1, and *Register of Cremations*, Crematorium at Rothwell Road Cemetery, Kettering.

120 *Market Harborough Advertiser and Midland Mail*, 27 December 1940, p. 1.

121 Ibid.

122 *Northampton Mercury*, 28 February 1941, p. 3.

123 *Market Harborough Advertiser and Midland Mail*, 27 December 1940, p. 5.

124 Ibid. Reginald Underwood was an author and musician, known for Bachelor's Hall (1934), Flame of Freedom (1936), Hidden Lights (1937), etc. He lived in Finedon, a few miles from Mary's home in Great Addington.

125 Ibid.

126 Ibid.

CHAPTER I

PEGGY writes:

"DEAREST JOAN,

"Rejoice with me for we have found a house! I was in the last stage of despair and had begun to think we should have to take to a tent, or a caravan. Percy didn't worry—you know he never worries about anything—but it was really getting serious, for one can't take four children to an hotel, or rooms, especially if one isn't a millionaire. We have to get out of this house in three months, and there seemed no prospect of finding another. We've been to see about umpteen hundred all over the country, because it doesn't matter to Perks where he lives; but they were all either beyond our limit in price or absolutely impossible. We saw this one advertised in *Country Life*—you know the sort of dream palace they portray—and sighed to think it would probably be priced at double what we could afford. But the tag 'must be sold, even at a nominal price' gave us a ray of hope and we went to see it the other day.

"My dear, we got it dirt cheap, and it is a bargain. Not ideal, or all my fancy painted for a house to live in, but well built, 'commodious,' which means plenty of good-sized rooms, nice kitchens and offices, a pleasant well-lighted room for Perks' studio, and so forth. Curiously enough nobody seemed to want it, and I must say the neighbourhood is not *too* attractive. It is on the outskirts of a country town with a few other villas scattered near. 'Villas!' I hear you say contemptuously. Oh yes, it's a villa right enough; you couldn't call it anything else honestly, though it was labelled 'a country house' in the advertisement. And it's about as commonplace as they make 'em. But it's a *house*, a home, and for that I am truly thankful.

"The only fly in the ointment is that there is no gas or electric light laid on—I expect that partly accounts for its cheapness—but we got used to oil in the last house we had, and we can have electricity put in as soon as we've got over the first expense. I always think there's something rather enchanting about lamps and candles; they shed such a soft, romantic light; and fortunately I kept our Perfection cooker when we came here.[1] It's cheaper than a gas one. Anyhow I mean to make the best of things, and there's a lovely big garden for the children to play in.

"The late owner, I am told, was a curmudgeon and much disliked by his neighbours because of the menagerie he kept, animals that were a continual annoyance to everybody near; goats and pigs that filled the ambient air with poisonous odours; dogs that barked incessantly day and night. No amount of threatening or persuasion had any effect on him; he was quite impervious to entreaty and, from all accounts, a little mad. For this his house was known in the neighbourhood as 'Hell Corner,' but its proper name is 'The Beeches,' from two fine ones in the garden.

"Well, I am grateful to the old boy for dying, anyhow, and for dying without a will, which is the probable cause of the house being thrown on the market and sold at a reasonable price. He might have left it to a sister's cousin's aunt on condition that she lived in it! But the nearest of kin is a bachelor cousin who has an estate of his own somewhere, and doesn't want it. So, praise Allah! we get it, and shall move in with all possible despatch. It

1 Perfection cooker: oil lamp stove.

must be redecorated (you never saw such wall-papers in your life!), but that ought not to take long. The children are wildly excited at the thought of going to live in the country, which they picture as a sort of Noah's Ark land, full of fascinating animals. Unfortunately for them, the goats have been sold and the dogs despatched. The latter were so savage with being always chained that nobody dared go near them.

"No more now, old thing. Let me hear from you soon and I'll tell you how we go on. We are going to the sale next week, to see if we can pick up any carpets, etc., cheap.

"Yours,

"PEGGY.

"P.S.—By the way, I believe the legatee cousin lives in your part of the world. His name is the same—Barker. Do you know anything of him?"

Joan replies:

"Hearty congratulations, old dear! I'm so glad you've found a house at last. May it prove a source of comfort and joy for many years to come, even if it *is* a villa, and commonplace. The old houses that look so enthralling in advertisements are often unsatisfactory to live in, dark and inconvenient and insanitary. But however ordinary it is, my dear, I'm sure you'll beautify it with your fine taste and Percy's help. I don't like the name 'Hell Corner' for you. You're too psychic and susceptible to suggestion. You'll be dreaming of demons and seeing them in the shadows! Don't I know you well, sweet Peg? But now that the 'curmudgeon' has departed this life, with all his sins upon him, no doubt the name will die out, and you will find the place a fairyland in which your own little sprites will revel. Bless them, and give them a hug all round from Aunty Joan.

"Do I know Daniel Barker? Just don't I! Why, he's our landlord and the most grasping old heathen who ever skinned a flint! He has put our rent up and up, on the flimsiest pretexts, till we are in despair, and won't do a thing to the house, which is literally *rotting*. He never gives a penny away and is cordially hated by everybody—a regular Scrooge. What a shame it is such hogs should inherit fat legacies! And what fools people are not to make wills! Did your old boy die suddenly? He couldn't have left his money to anyone who needed it less, or would do less good with it, than old Dan Barker. *He* ought to live in 'Hell Corner' if anyone did. No doubt he will before long—not in your house, but *down below!*"

CHAPTER II

THE family of Dacre consisted of Percy, husband and father, an illustrator of books and magazines with a small private income; Margaret, his wife; Gilbert, known as Gib, their eldest son, aged seven; Katherine, known as K., their eldest daughter, aged five; Felicia, known as Fliss, their second daughter, aged three and a half; and Hereward Percy, known as Billikin or the Hobgoblin, aged one year and ten months. They had a young nurse named Rosamond Joyce Boggs, known as Nanny, and a general servant of somewhat riper years, named Irene Melisande, but known as Cook, or Cookie. She preferred this title of honour to any other, as suggesting the chef of the establishment, and giving her higher standard in domestic service than that she actually possessed. A parlourmaid, housemaid, and "tweenie" were thereby implied, whereas she filled all these posts in her own discreet and highly capable person. Both maidens adored the children and had a certain affection for Percy and Peggy, who gave them every satisfaction.

They were a good-looking young couple. Percy was sufficiently tall, slender, darkish, and serene-looking, rarely out of temper, and fond of talking. Peggy was small, golden-haired, pretty, and animated; somewhat highly strung and nervous, looking more delicate than she really was, and also much younger, for she was thirty-four and might have been taken for twenty-four. They were instantly noted as strangers at the sale of furniture to which they came, and were regarded with much interest as the new owners and tenants of The Beeches. They had motored seventy miles that morning, rising at six o'clock to do so, but both looked fresh and smart, with the indefinable London air about them.

It did not take Peggy long to decide what she would like to buy and what she wouldn't have as a gift. The early Victorian pictures and furniture came under the last category, and she declared that, sooner than live with any one of them she would "die in a ditch." But there was one carpet and a dinner service she wanted, with some linen sheets and thick blankets, some glass, some brooms and brushes and saucepans and, quite new, rustless knives. All those Perks must bid for and—yes, certainly, an old worked pole-screen of quaint design, a duck of a thing that she knew at a glance was valuable. She must have that, whatever it fetched. It would go so well with their Jacobean chairs and other antiques that she and Percy had collected. He demurred. It was not a necessity, he said, and they couldn't afford just now to indulge in luxuries. But Peggy declared that she would rather go without the necessities than not have this treasure; adding: "One always wants useless things most. Whoever longed for an umbrella or a strong pair of boots?"

Others, apparently, shared her desire for the fire-screen, and the bidding for it ran high. With a red spot on either cheek Peggy took the matter out of her husband's hands and ran it up until opponents, one by one, gave in.

"Haven't I been a fool?" she whispered to Percy, and his "Rather!" was a dash of cold water.

"I had to have it, Perks."

"So I observe"

"Are you angry?"

"Furiously."

She glanced at him out of the corners of her eye and glimpsed the twinkle in his own.

"We can do without other things," she murmured.

"Exactly. A carpet, for instance. Bare boards are much healthier."

"I'd rather eat on the floor than lose that lovely thing. I'm sure it's going to bring us luck. Something inside me tells me so."

"Something inside you always does find an excuse for your most shameless actions," he said, imperturbably. "You do humbug your little self, don't you?"

"Yes, but not *you*," she retorted quickly, and they both laughed. It was true she could never humbug Percy. His love was great but by no means blind. They were standing just outside the door of the room where the selling was going on when this short dialogue took place.

"Can't you really afford the carpet now," she said, anxiously.

"Not if anyone wants it as badly as you did the screen," he said. "I've settled my price, and if it fetches more we'll have to buy a bit of cocoanut matting instead—that's all. One can't have everything in this world."

However, they did get the carpet and the dinner service, the mops and brooms and blankets and various other things, including a rather charming pseudo-Sheraton writing table, which Peggy swore was a real antique and felt sure it had a secret drawer in which she should find something wonderful. Percy declared that it had been made last year and was a clever fake, but he bought it all the same, at a moderate price. After all, he told himself, if it gave Peggy so much pleasure, what did it matter whether it was genuine or fake? He didn't care. Beauty was beauty to Percy; fashion and age were of no account. Peggy's whims were. He forked out willingly and had his reward in her childish joy. After all, he told himself, he had got the house much cheaper than he had expected.

They were standing together by a table in a room that looked on a pretty little garden pleasance, with a fountain in the middle of a round pool, and Percy was saying what a lovely mess the children would get themselves into playing there, when Peggy suddenly shivered through her slender body and ejaculated "Ugh!" He looked round and saw that she had turned pale.

"Only a goose walking over my grave," she replied with a grimace. "I had a queer sensation come over me, as if—as if—oh, you'll only laugh."

She paused.

"No—I won't. As if—what?"

"As if something icy cold had brushed past me."

"You're tired, my dear, and hungry. So am I, after that hurried lunch. We'll go back to the hotel and have a bursting tea. Come along. Theres nothing else we want, is there?"

A voice behind broke into their conversation and both paused involuntarily.

"Yes, it does seem dreadful, when we know how he would have hated it—having a lot of people in his house, poking his things about. Hardly anybody has seen the inside of it before. The blinds were always kept down in front of the house, you know, and every door locked and bolted. Have you seen the key basket? About two dozen keys, and it weighs a ton!" said the voice, and another took up the tale.

"Talk about turning in one's grave. I should think he must. Poor old thing! That's if he knows. It is to be hoped he doesn't."

"I don't feel sorry for him a bit," said the first voice. "Look how he treated that poor, faithful women who worked for him over twenty years and gave up everything, and every friend, she had in the world to make him comfortable. She must have led a dull, miserable life here, alone all day while he was at business or away. He used to go to London a lot. How beautifully she kept the house, too, not even a speck of dust under the carpets—did you notice? And then, after promising to provide for her, never leaving her a penny. And she's not the only one. The gardener, Judkins, and the other men who worked for him are very bitter about it. They say he gave them low wages, promising them they would get good legacies when he died. I call it really criminal of him not to make a will after telling them that—cheating the poor things."

"I suppose he didn't know he was going to die."

"Then he was a fool, as well as a knave! Does any man live for ever? And he was over seventy."

"They say he wasn't all there—very odd and queer in his ways. That might partly account for it. He certainly didn't behave like a sane man, from all I've heard; keeping dogs always chained up, like wild beasts, and never letting anyone inside his house. Would any man in his senses . . . "

The voices trailed off as the speakers went on to another room. Peggy and her husband had pretended to look at some old books on the table while they listened to this interesting conversation. They were making their way out when they heard a girl say with a light laugh: "Brrh! there's a dreary sort of feeling about this house somehow. I don't think I'd like to live here, would you? I'm sure I should always be seeing the old man grinning at me through the windows."

"Oh, don't, Nell. You give me the creeps," said another voice, and these, too, passed the door. Peggy clutched Percy's arm convulsively.

"Did you hear those people? Oh, Perks, I can't live here—I wish we hadn't bought the house."

"Because a lot of drivelling women talk piffle. Don't be an ass, Peg. We shall be as jolly as dogs here, you'll see. Come on."

"Those poor chained brutes couldn't have been very jolly!"

"Well, we shan't be chained, my dear. Let's get out of this stuffy place."

"I suppose I am rather an ass," said Peggy reflectively, as they walked down the short drive to the gate.

"A superlative one," he declared cheerfully. "And why not? The ass is a useful animal with lots of character."

"I don't see how one could love an ass."

"Ho! don't you? Well, I do."

She began to giggle. "You are the limit, Perks."

"I am that—and more," said Perks.

CHAPTER III

IT was a soaking day in the middle of September when Percy and Peggy Dacre entered their new home at Leatheringham. They had hoped to occupy it at least a month earlier, but, in such cases, man proposes and labour disposes. We all know what happens to houses whose landlords or tenants desire to have them redecorated. The work is promised to be completed by a certain date, but when that date arrives the work is hardly begun. Far be it from the writer of this veracious chronicle to lay any blame on anybody in particular. It may be the master decorator's fault; it may be the men's. We know the latter have an annoying little habit of beginning a job and then going off somewhere to finish another. "Variety's the spice of life," and they may find it monotonous to stick at one too long. Anyhow, there it is, and fine lessons in patience are the result thereof. Mr. and Mrs. Dacre chafed exceedingly, but some people may consider they were lucky in getting into their new home by September.

The loads of furniture had mostly been discharged by the time they arrived by car. A van stood in the road outside the house as they drew up, and two men were hauling unshapely objects out of it, in the rain, bearing a certain amount of gravel and mother earth with them from the garden into the house as they did so.

They had brought Cookie with them, and she sniffed at first sight of the place, but was reassured when she saw the large light kitchen, with its window looking out upon the garden. She appreciated, also, the nice scullery, with its copper and drying apparatus, and the big larder and pantry. Peggy had broken to her, as gently as possible, the regrettable absence of a gas-cooker, to which she had been accustomed, so she was spared the shock to her nerves. A char-lady, who had been recommended to Mrs. Dacre by the auctioneer who had sold them the house, had prepared a good fire in the Gargantuan kitchener, all polished up to distraction, and also in one of the reception-rooms and a bedroom; so the place, in spite of its chaos, did not look too dreary.

They had not, of course, brought the children, who were to be fetched, with Nanny, as soon as the new abode was prepared to receive them. A friend was keeping house in the meantime. Their absence did not tend to raise the spirits of the young couple, who were rarely parted from their small family and hated to have them out of their sight. But they had no time to mope, for there was much to do before darkness set in, and they were very busy till six o'clock, the time fixed for their evening meal. They had lunched on their way and had only a cup of tea when they got in; so they were ravenous, as well as very tired, when they sat down, in the kitchen, to a scratch meal of tinned tongue, eggs, bread and butter, and tea, which was all Cookie could provide for them. They pronounced it, by the way, the most delicious, satisfying, and enjoyable repast they had ever eaten!

There was very little they could do after dark, for they were not used to the comparatively dim light of lamps, so could not put down carpets, hang pictures and curtains, or do any of the hundred and one things necessary to the furnishing of a house. They could only go on unpacking certain precious pieces of furniture that had been wrapped round with straw and sacking—fix up more comforts in the bedrooms for themselves and Cookie, and stow away the contents of a packing-case full of household linen in the hot cupboard by the bathroom.

By the time that was done Peggy began to feel very worn out and depressed. The gloom of the house; the moaning of wind and continuous beat of rain on the creepers outside; the strange shadows thrown by the small oil-lamp they worked by, all preyed on her mind and gave her an eerie feeling of boding ill-fortune. Percy, who, although an artist, had nothing of the 'artistic temperament,' was unperturbed as usual, and seemed to regard everything annoying or inconvenient as part of the picnic—he called it a picnic. When he had done as much work as he wanted to do, he just wandered about, with his pipe in his mouth and his hands in his pockets, making whimsical comments upon everything and chaffing Peggy for getting heated and worried.

"You're a beast, Perks," she exclaimed, after one of his gibes. "You always laugh at me. But I don't care what you say. I feel sure something horrid is going to happen. Probably the children have caught measles. I heard that Bobby Baines fell with them the day after that party they went to. And if so, we shan't get them here for weeks and weeks."

"Well, they haven't got measles yet. Give 'em a chance."

"Just lend a hand with this chest of drawers, lazy-bones. I wonder which room the old boy slept in," Peggy switched off, as they pushed the chest into the place she designated for it. "I hope it wasn't this one."

"Ssh!" he said, looking round mysteriously, and speaking in a creepy whisper: "Don't let him hear you speak of him so disrespectfully."

Oh, be quiet, Perks! Do you want to make me scream? You always scoff, but you'll see——"

"I don't mind what *I* see," he said, "as long as *you* don't see anything. I'm not afraid of spooks. Let 'em all come! What a filthy state we're in, aren't we? I think I'll have a bath."

"No you don't," said Peggy, with emphasis. "I'm not going to be left alone a minute. If you have a bath, I'll sit in the bathroom."

"I don't mind. There's no false modesty about me," he observed blandly.

But he did not take his bath then, and they went down to the room they had decided to make their morning-room, as it faced east and looked on the pretty little fountain court.

While they had been upstairs Cookie and Mrs. Tubb had made it habitable, with two easy chairs, a bright lamp, and big fire. There was no carpet down yet, but they had found a Persian rug and laid it down by the fire. It looked cosy.

"That Cookie of ours is a pearl of great price," remarked Percy, as he stretched his tired legs to the blaze. "By the way, Peg, who thought of the oil? I suppose it was the char-lady. I'm sure you didn't."

"Oh, didn't I?" said Peggy, making a face at him. Then she laughed, for of course she hadn't thought about the oil. "I'm afraid you don't think I'm a pearl of great price."

"Ten a penny, more likely! But one can't have everything, and you have golden hair and onyx eyes and a pearly skin and a ruby mouth, so I must fain be content."

"Go to! You know perfectly well I'm a miracle among housewives and think of your every comfort. Say, Perks, when can we get electric light in? How long will it take?"

"Star of my soul, haven't I told you it has to be brought two miles and will cost a fortune. Now do be a decent fellow and don't worry your poor bread-winner for impossibilities. Do you want to see him in the Bankruptcy Court?"

"It will be a saving in the end, Perks."

"I don't think so!"

"It would. It would save doctor's bills. The children will be always tumbling downstairs, and I shall have a nervous fever."

"Then you will go to the hospital—free ward."

"Don't be a beast. You must work a little harder and send things out—or charge more."

"If I charged half as much for my drawings I could sell twice as many!" He chuckled over this quotation from *Punch*. "All in good time, my Blessing. We'll have electric light when I am appreciated at my true worth and all the editors and advertisers in the world are at my feet."

"They would be now if they only knew what was good," said Peggy, who had immense faith in her husband's talent.

"They never do, my dear. They needs must love the lowest when they see it. But no matter. A day will come when they *shall* hear me—I mean, see me, in posters a mile high beautifying the landscape from Land's End to John o' Groat's. I've an idea for one now—a rapturous Robinson Crusoe, of gigantic size, finding a footprint on his desert island of the Matchless Corn-curing Shoe. I think of turning my talent to advertisements altogether, Peg, and chucking the other work. It will pay me better, and when a man has a wife clamouring for electric extravagances and so forth, he must prostitute his genius in order to——"

He was not permitted to finish the sentence. The clamouring wife was at that instant on his knees, with one hand over his slanderous mouth and the other rumpling his curly dark hair. And the discussion came to an end.

CHAPTER IV

THE next few days were spent in a hectic muddle. Cookie came to Peggy every hour of the day with the enquiry: "I s'pose you don't remember, mum, where we packed—so-and-so?" And Peggy's invariable answer was, "I really don't, Cookie." Or it would be Peggy who asked the question and received the same reply. She and Cookie had packed most of the small things, china, glass, silver, linen, etc., not trusting them to the men who were ready to undertake this as part of their job, and the result was chaos, as, upon arrival, their minds seemed blank on the subject. However, they found everything in time, and got the house into some kind of order.

A little room that had once been a conservatory, with a glass roof, had been converted by the late owner into a place where he kept stores during the Great War, his nervous soul being consumed by the dread of starvation. On discovery he had had to pay rather heavily for this infringement of regulations and the room had been since disused. It was ideal as a studio for Percy, and when a thick felt covering had been laid on the tessellated floor, and a marvellously heat-dispelling oil stove had been found for a corner, it was not too comfortless. Not that Percy demanded much in the way of comfort. He was, perhaps, the most easily-pleased man in this respect the world has ever known; but he could not, of course, draw with frozen fingers. The room led out of the morning-room, where a fire was always kept burning, and, with the door open between, shed some of its warmth into the other. On sunny days the glass roof gave it the temperature of a conservatory.

There were, besides, two big rooms for dining-room and drawing-room, but these did not come into everyday use until the house was finished and everything normal.

Peggy's prognostication about the measles was not fulfilled. They received good news of the children's health and arranged for them to come in less than a week after entering the new home. But the night before Percy was to fetch them something happened.

Percy went out to post a letter at a pillar-box standing at the end of the road, and when he came back he found Peggy standing in the doorway. She ran out to meet him, as he came through the gate and up the circular carriage drive.

"Oh, what a long time you've been!" she cried. "Did you hear the dogs?"

"What dogs?" he asked, adding hastily: "Oh, those; yes, of course I did. Who wouldn't? They are at that big house round the corner. I should say an Airedale by the bark, or two."

"Perks, you know they have only lap-dogs at the corner house. Besides——"

"Probably got a visitor. Dogs hate strange houses, you know. I think we must have another dog, Peg, and give our neighbours a bit of their own back."

"Oh, no, Percy, I couldn't—after poor darling Micky."

Her voice broke. Micky had been their Irish terrier, deeply beloved and recently defunct. They had decided they couldn't bear to have another in his place.

Peggy's fears were allayed as soon as Percy said he had heard the barking, though a small suspicion lurked in her mind as to the validity of his suggestion than an Airedale, or other deep-mouthed hound, was visiting at the corner house. She did not suspect the truth, that Percy had heard no barking whatever, and his unveracious statement was due to a quick perception of her superstitious fears. He had heard her say, more than once, that it would not surprise her if the ghosts of those poor murdered dogs gave tongue, and when he saw her white face and terror-stricken eyes at the door, jumped to a conclusion. She fancied she had heard them. Percy gave his wife credit for sufficient imagination to create bogies and left it at that. His faith in things unseen might have been represented by a cipher. The only way to squash her terrors was to pretend he had heard dogs at the corner house, so, like a good, comforting husband, mindful only of his wife's welfare, he lied cheerfully and decisively.

It was silent enough now, as they went into the drawing-room and sat down again by the fire. Not a sound disturbed the stillness, save the steady drip of rain on the creepers outside and an occasional gust of wind against the windows. It was a very wet autumn that year, and had rained, on and off, nearly the whole week. They found the silence rather oppressive—at least Peggy did. Percy was rarely oppressed, or depressed, by anything. They had come from town and were not yet used to country quiet. Even in the village home they had occupied some years previously, they heard the whistles and shunting of trains not far off; the talk of labourers dragging heavy boots on the road outside; the lowing of bereaved cows and other country noises. But here, well outside the town and not on a main road, an occasional motor-car passing, or a cock crowing, was all they ever heard at night.

Their talk drifted, grew fragmentary, and died away in gusts, like the wind outside. It was as if they both listened for something, as, in fact, they did. Percy longed for a dog to bark. He thought it quite possible that he might have heard one when he was out, with the ears of his head, which very often did not communicate to his mind. Absorbed in his art or his thought, he was apt to be oblivious to noises. Peggy, on the other hand, listened with dread, fearing to hear again the thing that had driven her, in a panic, from the warm room to the front door; when she simply dared not remain alone another moment!

But no dog barked to oblige Percy or terrify her. They sat and listened, Percy smoking and Peggy knitting. Suddenly she said:

"How thankful I shall be when the children come! It's awful without them. For goodness sake, let us do something, Perks—play picquet, cribbage, or bezique, or patience, rather than sit here like two mummies in a tomb."

"Anything you like, my Angel. It does seem queer, certainly, not to know the imps are up above," he agreed. They often called their children "the imps," which Percy said was good old English for "child." "But really, Peg, it's all fancy about missing them at this time of night, when they're always in bed and asleep."

"I *do* miss them, though," she retorted, "and so do you. We know they're not here, and when they are overhead we just feel as if they were in the room. Bless the darlings. I do hope they will not develop measles as soon as they get here. You must be sure and cover them up well, Perks, in that long drive."

"There's nothing like being prepared for the worst," He laughed: "I wonder if there ever was such a fertile imagination as yours, Peg. Although you always have all the luck. I'm prepared to take you on at anything you like."

"Luck! You know perfectly well that I never have any decent cards, and that it is only by consummate skill I ever manage to wrest a game from you," declared Peggy, as she got out the cards. "What is it to be?"

"I think piquet. It's the most intellectual. And for highbrows like us, therefore, the most suitable."

"Speak for yourself. I don't pretend to be a highbrow, and bezique is good enough for me."

"Oh yes, I know why. Because you always get the royal sequence and double bezique."

"And you always have a huitième when it is your major hand."

So they pretended to squabble; it was part of the fun, and they never failed to accuse each other of "all the luck." Finally they tossed up, which game they should play, and after he had won for piquet, they agreed upon cribbage!

But although they played, complained of their cards, exulted over each other with brutal candour, or chattered gaily, all the while, they still listened. They listened in bed until they fell asleep!

CHAPTER V

THE weather was so bad next day, simply pouring in torrents, that Peggy, much as she longed for her darlings, would not let Percy start in it. They waited all the morning and part of the afternoon, hoping it would clear up, but it did not, and a telegram was sent, postponing the journey till next day. An hour after this was despatched the rain ceased and the sun came out; but it was then rather late to set forth for a seventy-mile drive, so the disconsolate pair consoled themselves as best they could for another dreary day without "the imps."

A week of strenuous labour, in which all hands were employed—including those of Mr. Barker's gardener, whom Percy had taken on, and the char-lady, a somewhat slovenly person, whose chief characteristic was a willingness to oblige—had set the new house in fair order, so that there was nothing left for Percy and Peggy to do in it. The carpets were all laid, the book-shelves filled, the curtains and pictures hung, the day-nursery attractively furnished. It was the largest of the bedrooms, with a big bow window, and its choice for a nursery had rather shocked Cookie, who thought it ought to be the "spare room."

"It would make such a lovely spare room, mum," she had said, "with that beautiful wardrobe and all," referring to a piece of furniture Percy had taken over at the sale, to supply a deficiency of cupboard room."

"You are right, Cookie, as usual," Percy had observed blandly: "It *would* make a bee-ewtiful spare room, fit to entertain royalty in. But, you see, we're not going to entertain royalty, or anyone else, to speak of, so shan't want a spare room; only a sort of cubby-hole to poke people into if they insist on coming to stay with us. Our offspring, as you have probably observed by now, are our first consideration, and they must have a room they can exercise their legs in when the weather's too bad for them to go out."

Cookie had forced a smile and remarked that she supposed he must have his joke; but, in the families where she'd lived before, visitors were always given the best room in the house. To which Percy had replied that he was quite aware he had not been properly brought up, but it couldn't be helped now.

Into this room the husband and wife made pilgrimages several times that day, to see that it was as perfect as their ideal had planned, or if anything had been omitted which could possibly add to the joy or well-being of the children. They looked at it now with wistful eyes—at the dado of lovely animals; the bright parrot hanging on a ring from the ceiling, with several pretty balloons; at the rocking horse, and pen, and doll's house, the big box of toys in a corner, the low chairs and stools, the safety guard by the fire, dainty curtains and bowl of flowers on the table by the window. On that table were the deep plates with pictures in them, and their mugs on which each name was inscribed; Gilbert, Katherine, Felicia, Hereward. And, as her eyes fell on these, Peggy exclaimed:

"Why, Perks, we've forgotten Billikin's 'pusher.' How stupid of me!"[2]

The two younger children used these lately invented "pushers"

---

[2] To deter small children from touching food with their fingers, a 'pusher' was used to push food onto a spoon or fork.

instead of forks, and one of them had disappeared in the packing. Peggy had intended to buy another, and had forgotten it.

"That's all right, we'll go into the town and buy it now, after tea," said Percy. "And—tell you what, Peg, we may as well have dinner down there, and go to the pictures afterwards. It'll be better than mooning about here, thinking of the imps and settling to nothing."

"What about Cookie, left alone in the house? She may be nervous?"

"Not she. Why should she be?"

"I should be."

"Because you're a goose is no reason why Cookie should be. Ask her if she minds. I know what she'll say."

He was right. Cookie scoffed at the idea of minding a few hours alone. So they went off cheerfully, to have a festive evening in the town; the nice little dinner Peggy had planned, thinking Percy would be hungry after driving all day, was postponed till the next night. They bought the "pusher" and several other things they wanted—or thought they wanted—then they dined at the "White Hart" and went to see a cow boy film at the Picture Palace. They giggled softly all through the sentimental parts, but Peggy shed a surreptitious tear over the mother whose infant son, stolen by the evil-minded villain, was restored by the bronco-busting hero. He was rather a darling, that baby, Peggy whispered to Perks, although a bit long in the leg and mature of teeth for a year-old infant.

It was a clear, bright night, lighted by many stars, when they came out, and, as they neared the outskirts of the town, they could smell the sharp scent of fallen leaves. They stepped out briskly, laughing over the absurdities of the melodramatic film they had seen, and had reached their house when Peggy suddenly stopped and clutched Percy's arm.

"Who's that?" she whispered, "looking over our gate?"

"Don't be silly," said her husband, dragging her on; "there's nobody looking over the gate. It's the shadow of the fir tree. There, I can see it too—moving with the breeze. You little goose."

Peggy drew a deep breath. The figure she had seen vanished at their approach.

"Percy, I did see some one," she said, "an oldish man in a bowler hat. Didn't you really see some one, Percy? I hope he's not lurking in the bushes."

"There's no one here, my foolish Fay, or I should have seen him. What a start you gave me! Do you want to see your poor Perks fall in a fit? You're always giving him frightful shocks when he least expects 'em. Some day you'll frighten him into an untimely grave, and then—I give you fair warning—he'll haunt you."

"Don't, Perks. I won't have you joke about such things."

They went in. The house was dark, silent, and smelly; for the lamp in the hall was low and going out. Cookie had thought its oil would last another night and omitted to fill it. She had gone to bed, but had made up a good fire in the breakfast-room and set out sandwiches, cocoa, and milk, with a small saucepan and kettle in the fender. The lamp in this room was all right, and they sat down cosily to eat sandwiches with good appetite, for their walk had made them hungry.

"You might just go and put the kitchen lamp in the hall, Perks," said Peggy, after a while. "You'll find it on the dresser."

"Why bother?" he said. "We can find our way upstairs in the dark and there's a light on the landing."

"I hate going upstairs in the dark," Peggy pouted. "You might do as I ask, Perks."

"Have I ever refused to do any behest of yours, my precious poppet?"

He rose lazily and went out. Peggy gazed at the fire. What a dear he was! When he came back she said:

"How thankful I shall be to have the children here."

It was not a new and original remark. She had made it several times a day for the last week.

"I suppose you think they will protect you from old men in bowler hats, who look over gates," he observed, expecting a quick retort and a delicious little squabble. But she only laughed, and said, with a heavenly smile:

"Of course they will, the darlings!"

CHAPTER VI

PERCY started off early next morning and returned about half-past four in the afternoon. There was rapture at The Beeches when his car, with its precious load, drove through the gateway to the door, where an impatient woman stood waiting. It seemed to her an age since she had held Billikin in her arms and heard his delicious "Mummie—Mummie!" The elder children were frantically excited over the new house and rampaged all over it as soon as they entered, finally tearing round the garden and into the large yard with its row of stable doors on one side and dog kennels on the other. These kennels were so curiously made, and of such a large size, that only one had been sold at the sale. The children found them full of interest.

"Bow-wow gone 'way," Fliss observed, and thereupon inserted her small person into one of the kennels, from which she had to be withdrawn by the tail of her coat.

"Where did they go, Mummie?" K. asked; and Gib exclaimed, "Wouldn't it be lovely if they were all here now, to play with us?" He added, in a mournful tone: "What could have induced people to get rid of nice dear dogs? I wish they hadn't."

"You see, darling, the gentleman who lived here died, and nobody else wanted them," said his mother.

"Where have they gone then?" he asked.

This was a poser. The children were not to know the dogs had been destroyed.

"I expect they were sold," Peggy suggested mendaciously.

"You'll buy some more, won't you, Daddy?" said K.

"When my ship comes home," was the reply. "We'll have a perfect menagerie then—dogs and cats and rabbits and goats and pigs and poultry—and other caged birds."

The children looked at him, thoughtfully, and Gib said: "When do you expect your ship, Daddy?"

"Can't say—to a week," responded Percy. "We must hope for the best, Gib."

"We can pretend, that's one thing," observed Gib, "can't we, K.? We'll pretend there's dogs in these kennels, shall we? And we can play at being dogs ourselves. Bow-wow-wow."

He gave a fair imitation of a bark, but Peggy frowned and stopped him.

"Don't do that, Gib," she said sharply. "It might . . . annoy people." Somehow, the sound sent a little shiver down her spine.

After tea the two elder children, after spending a few minutes inspecting their nursery, tore all over the house again, returning to their mother every few minutes with ecstatic announcements of discoveries.

"Oh, I say, Mummie, there's such a lovely cupboard in the attic, under the roof!" Or, "There's such good places for hide-and-seek in this house, Mummie. You can run right round by the back staircase and get home." Or, "Do you know there's a jolly little tap, quite low down, in the bathroom!"

Fliss and little Billikin were, however, tired out, and could hardly be undressed before they were fast asleep. The other children were soon ready to follow them, and Nanny, too, went to bed early. In the silence of the house Peggy and Percy sat, after dinner, talking over their precious flock and making plans for their future.

"I'm afraid Gib will develop into a writer of fiction," Percy said. "He makes up things out of his own head already, and is always 'pretending.' "

"K. loves drawing. I expect she will follow in your footsteps."

"Poor child! It is to be hoped not. But we needn't worry about Billikin, that's one comfort. His career is mapped out."

"What' that?"

"A clown. Either of the circus variety or the music-hall type. He's the most humorous imp I've ever seen and has a gutta-percha face.[3] Oh, he'll do all right. As for Fliss."

"She'll be a dancer. You can't keep her still."

"She takes after her dear mamma—all nerves and jumps and quick changes."

"Traducer!"

The discussion went on, more or less, all the evening: sometimes serious, oftener chaff and jesting. It was about ten o'clock when Peggy stopped in the middle of her speech—and, holding up her hand, listened.

"What's that?" she ejaculated, "one of the children calling."

A faint voice came through the thick walls and ceilings: "Mummie! Mummie!"

"It's Gib," cried Peggy, and flew upstairs.

She bounced into Nanny, who came from the night nursery. The two older children slept in a little room leading out of Peggy's.

Gib was sitting up in bed, with excited eyes.

"I heard the dogs barking," he said. "Did you hear them, Mummie? They must have run away and come back. Dogs do come back to their old homes, you know. They find out the way, somehow. Listen!"

---

[3] Gutta-percha: natural rubber.

A trickle, as of icy water, ran down Peggy's spine. She saw Nanny's face, with wide eyes, staring at her from a glass opposite, on which the light from the landing fell through the open door.

"Nonsense, darling, you've been dreaming," she said. "Now lie down and go to sleep again, like a good boy, or you'll wake K. If there had been any barking, Daddy and I would have heard it. You didn't hear a dog, did you, Nanny?" She turned to the girl behind her.

"No, 'm, not a sound."

"It wasn't *one* dog; it was lots," declared Gib, emphatically. "Six or seven I should think. And K. heard them too, didn't you, K.?"

K. was now rubbing her eyes in the little bed on the other side of the room.

"I fought I heard somefing," she murmured, "but it might have been a cow or a sheep or a pig or a . . . " her voice trailed off. She was half asleep.

"You are really a naughty boy to wake your little sister," said Peggy, severely. "Let me hear no more of this nonsense. You know perfectly well that there are no dogs here. You saw the empty kennels this afternoon. You're just pretending—making it up. You know you are."

Gib was silent a few moments, turning the matter over in his mind. "P'raps I was," he observed then; "or p'raps I dreamed there was dogs. But it seemed real—it really did, Mummie, and it wakened me right up. Dreams are funny things," he ended reflectively.

"Now be a good boy and go to sleep," his mother said, kissing the little dark head that snuggled down in the pillow again.

"I expect he's been over-tired and over-exited," she added to Nanny, as they went out of the room. "And he had rather a big supper. I'm sorry you were disturbed. You see, the children don't know that the dogs have been destroyed, and I expect Gib brooded over them and thought how they might come back till he persuaded himself he heard them. You won't tell the children they're dead, will you?"

"No fear! It would break their little hearts—they're that tender-hearted, and love animals. But I may tell Cookie, mayn't I, 'm? Or does she know?"

"Yes, she does. But I told her not to say anything to you, in case the children asked about them and you wouldn't know what to say. It was a pity we told them at first there were dogs and goats here, but we didn't know they had been despatched until afterwards."

"It does seem a shame to have killed the poor dogs," said the girls, indignantly. "Why did they do such a cruel thing, mum?"

"They were so savage that no one dare go near them, and they disturbed the whole neighbourhood, day and night."

"I don't think much of people who are afraid of dogs," remarked Nanny, contemptuously. "They might easily have been tamed with kindness."

"Of course they might, poor brutes! But it's done now and can't be helped."

"Well, if I'd done such a cruel thing as that, I should expect the dogs to haunt me all my life," said Nanny, turning towards her room.

Peggy shrank, and exclaimed sharply: "Don't say silly things." She went downstairs, shivering, as if with cold, and Nanny went into the night nursery.

"Well, what was the trouble?" her husband asked, looking up from a book.

"Perks, what do you think it was?"

Her eyes were dilated with fear. She came closer to him and put her foot on the fender, for she felt chilled through.

"Haven't an idea."

"I shan't tell you unless you promise not to scoff."

"I never scoff. Go on."

"I found Gib sitting up in bed, wildly excited, because he said the dogs had come back. *He heard them barking.*"

"Gosh!"

He stared at her, with a puzzled expression for a moment. Then he laughed.

"The little monkey! Don't look so tragic, Peg. What did you do with him. Give him a good smack?"

"Yes, of course. We always smack our children, don't we?" she replied, with biting irony. "What would you have done?"

"Told him not to be silly, and go to sleep."

"Which I did. I told him there were no dogs, and that he had been dreaming. And such in his faith in Mummie that he believed me. But he *did* hear those dogs, Percy. And I heard them too."

"Tosh!"

"It wasn't tosh—I did. And I did before."

"There are dogs at the corner house—as I said before."

"But we never hear them, and they are only lap-dogs, kept in at night."

"My Heart's Pride and Desire, do be reasonable. If there had been dogs barking, I should have heard them."

"It doesn't follow. In the first place, I may be able to hear what you cannot. In the second place, you often don't hear sounds that I do, when your mind is concentrated on something else. You know you're not sensitive to noise."

"Bless my soul! If there'd been noise enough to wake a child, do you think I shouldn't hear it? Is thy servant a deaf adder?"

"There's none so deaf as those who won't hear," Peggy quoted.

He laughed. "Well, never mind, old lady. Come and sit down sociably and I'll read you what Bernard Shaw says about——"

"I don't want to hear what Bernard Shaw says. He's a sceptic and a scoffer like yourself."

She stood looking down at the fire for a minute or two in silence. Then she went on:

"It doesn't matter how you scoff, Percy, or what you say. I am perfectly certain this house is haunted. I suspected it when we came to the sale. I *knew* it the very first night we were here. The only thing now is, how long can I stand it?"

With that she sat down and took up her work, a little frock she was embroidering for Fliss, but her hands were so cold she could hardly hold the needle. She wanted to go to bed, but dared not go up alone and wouldn't ask Percy to go too. So they sat some time in silence.

CHAPTER VII

WHEN she awoke next morning Peggy was ashamed of her fears the night before, and agreed with Percy that she was a silly little goose. She had a busy day, and a very happy one, with her children. They loved the new house and garden; the day was fine and they were able to be out of doors a good deal. In the afternoon Peggy had her first caller, a nice woman who told her of a small Kindergarten where her own children went, not too far off, and Peggy decided, on the spot, to send Gib and K. there at the next half-term. Mrs. Palmer was not a gossip, and she did not say much about the late owner of The Beeches, except that he was very eccentric and unpopular. But she sat long after tea chatting about the town's many activities, its churches, chapels, and institutions generally.

There were, she said, three Churches of England, one Roman Catholic, about seven chapels, a Friends' Meeting House, a Salvation Army Barracks, and a Brotherhood Hall. There were Boys' and Girls' Brigades and bands of different sorts and sizes; also an orchestral society and another for chamber music. For amusements the town had a large picture palace and several other halls devoted to the same purpose; a dancing class and occasional *Thé Dansants* at the White Hart Assembly Rooms.[4]

Did Mrs. Dacre sing? The choral and operatic societies would heartily welcome her as a member. Did she like acting? The A. D. S. would like to have her in it. Did she play golf and badminton? She

---

[4] *Thé Dansants*: tea dance.

must join the Golf and Badminton Clubs. And Mrs. Palmer hoped she would help in their sewing meetings for the Social Service League, or at the Infants' Welfare Centre. She invited Peggy to join the Small Bridge Club just started among friends, the first meeting to be at her house next Monday. Peggy accepted with pleasure. She loved bridge and she liked meeting fresh people. It seemed a good way of entering into the social life of the town.

She felt a trifle bewildered after the good lady had left, and the impression Percy received of her visit was something in the nature of an avalanche. He thanked his lucky stars that he had been out when Mrs. Palmer called, as he found Peggy's account of her sufficiently overwhelming. But he was quite willing for his wife to enter into some of the town's social and benevolent activities. They would keep her over-imaginative mind from brooding, he concluded, and the exercise would keep her healthy. He was no mean golf-player, and agreed to join the Golf and Badminton Clubs forthwith. Also, he promised to take her to the next *Thé Dansant*, for they both loved dancing.

Other callers came the next day, and the next, thick and fast. Life for Peggy began to hum. It was soon discovered that she was charming and ready to enter into everything with a zest. Her husband had a certain fame as an artist, in *Punch* and other papers, and when the men of the town found that he gave himself no airs and was a good sportsman, they chummed up with him and put him up as a member of their clubs, including the Bowling Club, which was a great centre of the town's masculinity in summer-time, and where a good deal of card-playing was done in the winter.

Altogether the young couple seemed in danger of having all their time swallowed up in social engagements; but they both resolved not to let themselves be sucked too far in, as they really loved their own fireside and to be alone together. They were not at all a fashionable and modern couple, the Dacres.

As soon as she had everything nice in her house Peggy looked forward to a visit from her dearest friend and schoolfellow, Joan Millis, and she found a good deal to do before this end could be achieved. A hundred and one things always crop up to be done in a house long after one fancies it is all in order; the little touches that make for beauty and comfort, which only a woman ever realizes. And where there are children, "four rumbustious imps," as Percy called them, always wanting Mummie and never content to remain, as good children ought, in their own little domain, it is not easy to get on with any kind of work. So the weeks passed into October and through into November before Peggy could invite her friend to stay.

The strange terrors that had perturbed her at first did not recur in these weeks. Gib slept well, his dreams undisturbed by any more barking of dogs or other hallucinations, and all four children were in the pink of health. Peggy concluded that she had been the victim of her own imagination and a run-down nervous system played upon by what she had heard of old Barker. It was all nonsense, she told herself, about the house being haunted. It was a nice, homely, commonplace sort of house; not a bit the kind in which any ghost would disport itself. Like most of us, she visualized the haunted house as of the Moated Grange type—a place where awful crimes had been committed. If only The Beeches had electric light, or even incandescent gas, she reflected, it would be prosaic to the last degree. But it was this queer, glimmering, old-world light of lamp and candle that threw strange shadows into corners and lent a kind of mysterious atmosphere to the house at night. It did not look the same place in the daytime.

"You know what a little fool I am, Joey," she wrote to her friend: "When I first came here, I was always fancying I heard strange noises, and there were odd things that happened, as I told you. But that is all in the past and I am getting quite fond of our 'little 'Ole' as Percy calls it. It's not romantic or picturesque, or anything of that kind, but it is habitable and comfy, now that we've got things straight and can manage the oil better. It was awful at first, continually diffusing unholy smells, and shedding showers of sooty matter all over the furniture. I am afraid Cookie risked her immortal soul more than once in bad language, and I know I did. But now I am getting rather to like lamplight. It doesn't try the eyes, when you sit near enough to it, and these new Aladdin mantles are a godsend.[5] When will you come and sample it? I'm ready for you now, at any time.

"Perks is working like two men and a boy now—lots of orders and full of ideas, as usual. He really is a clever pig, is Perks. I enclose two small sketches of the Imps making muddy messes in the garden. There's a little round pond with a fountain in it, which they adore, and never want to leave it. I wonder why water has always such a fascination for children. It's curious, when they also love dirt so much. They are never so happy as when they are dirty, I'm sure.

"Yours,

"PEGGY.

Joan replied by return of post, saying she would come next week, and Peggy began to plan mild gaieties for her; among them

5 The incandescent mantle was placed over an Aladdin lamp burner and produced a much brighter light than a bare flame.

a bridge drive, which she found to be a very popular form of entertainment in the town. She had been invited to one, in which she was the winner of the second prize, and now resolved to invite all the women who had called upon her to one at her own house. Percy demurred, begging to be left in peace for a while and declaring that if a lot of chattering women invaded his house he would go on the spree and not return until they had cleared out. But she knew him too well to believe that. Perks would never let her down. She laughed at the threat and thoroughly enjoyed making her arrangements, buying the presents, engaging the tables, and writing her invitation cards.

She also made Percy promise to drive them over to the theatre at the county town one night, and took tickets for a subscription dance at the Mason's Hall. With all this to occupy her the week passed happily, and she had only one jar, which pulled her up rather sharply and started again the sense of something malign and uncanny she had felt in the house from the first day she entered it.

CHAPTER VIII

PEGGY was playing with the children in the nursery the day before Joan Millis came, when Cookie came in and said there was "a lady" in the kitchen who wished to speak to her.

"What kind of a lady? Did she give her name?" Peggy asked.

"Yes'm. It is Miss Susan Cleaver. She says she used to live here."

The housekeeper! Peggy's mind jumped to this conclusion, though she did not remember having heard the woman's name. She said nothing to Cookie, however, except that she would see Miss Cleaver in the morning-room.

When Miss Susan Cleaver entered Peggy saw a tall, spare woman, with a nervous face and large anxious eyes, quietly dressed in a navy serge coat and skirt, with a superannuated hat perched on the top of closely coiled, greying hair.

"I hope you will excuse my intrusion, ma'am," she said, "but I heard that you sometimes needed extra help in the house, and I thought there was no harm in asking if you would employ me. I should be very glad to oblige you in that way, if you are not suited."

"Well," Peggy hesitated a little. "I have some one who comes in to help occasionally, though I can't say I am suited, exactly. She isn't very capable, or clean, but as she came at first and did her best, I hardly like to take anyone in her place. Otherwise, I should have been pleased to accept your services."

She had, indeed, been wondering how she could get rid of Mrs. Tubb, as charwoman, without hurting her feelings; for the woman was very slatternly and inefficient.

For a few moments her visitor said nothing; only fixed her

large mournful eyes on Peggy's face and moistened her lips.

"I know Mrs. Tubb," she said at last. "And you'll forgive me for saying, ma'am, that she is little or no good, because she scamps things so.[6] . . . In fact, if I may speak plainly, I heard you were dissatisfied with her, and that is why I came. When I lived here, I employed her to help clean once or twice and found she was no help, as I had to do her work over again."

Peggy called to mind the exquisite cleanliness of the house at the sale, which she had heard the subject of comments by housewives on all sides, and wavered.

"There's such a thing," she suggested, "as being too particular. I am no slave to my house, though, of course, I like to see things kept clean."

The woman sighed. A little catch of a sigh.

"It is easy to see ma'am, from the look of your rooms, that you want everything kept nice," she said, humbly, as her cavernous eyes roved round the apartment. Peggy felt a spasm of pity for her and asked her to sit down.

"I understand you have lived here," she observed.

"Yes ma'am. I was Mr. Barker's housekeeper for twenty-two years."

"I have heard of you. And I must say that all I have heard was greatly to your credit."

There came a shine of tears into the large eyes. Peggy went on talking to save her a reply to this compliment.

"Have you been unable to get another situation yet?" she asked. "It ought to be easy enough in your case. Such good"—she was going to say "servants" but changed the word—"such good

---

[6] Scamp: to give short measure.

managers and workers are rare indeed. Perhaps I could find you an engagement among my friends."

"You are very good, ma'am, and thank you kindly for the offer, but I am not wishing for another situation at present, unless it is in this town. I cannot leave Leatheringham."

"Is there any reason for that? Do you mind telling me?" Peggy asked, with a sudden thirst for more knowledge of this strange personality, who intrigued her curiously. There was a look of character about her, and a suggestion of tragedy. The woman's story was, indeed, enough to suggest this, without her tense and strained expression. For is not disappointment tragic when it is accompanied by disillusion and confidence betrayed? The 'curmudgeon,' as she privately called old Barker, had failed to keep his word, had allowed a good and faithful servant to go unrewarded and, wounding her to the heart, had left her helpless before the burden of years.

To her surprise the woman seemed to read her thoughts.

"Yes, there is a reason, ma'am," she said; "a good reason. I mean to stay about here until I have solved a mystery and taken away a stigma from a good man's character. I dare say you've been told I've been ill-treated, and so I have, in a way. But you must not think that Mr. Barker was to blame. Oh no! He was a strange man and very peculiar in his ideas—as nobody knows better than me who lived with him so long, and understood him as well as anyone ever could. And even I couldn't quite get to the bottom of his queer mind. He didn't trust anybody, and he thought everyone was against him but me. He was secret and sly in his ways, and a bit selfish, like men get who have no one but themselves to think of. He never seemed to care what people said or thought about him, but he *did* care really. He brooded on it and thought everyone was unneighbourly till he hated all his neighbours. He wouldn't let me leave the house a moment unless he was in it, and always waited in fear of being robbed. That was why he kept savage dogs—to scare people."

She moistened her lips and went on, with a rising colour in her thin, sallow cheeks.

"But, for all that, ma'am, he was a good man, and a kind man at heart. He never had an evil thought, and he always treated me respectful; not like a menial, or in any way familiar. He always said he should provide for my old age, as I had served him well, and he meant it, I'm sure. I never heard him speak anything but the truth; he was an honourable man—even those who didn't like him would say that. He didn't give me high wages, and I didn't ask for them. I was mistress here, and I liked the post. He always said 'As long as I'm alive, you can have all you want here, and you don't need to save because I've provided for you.' Those were the very words he used, and he used them only a week before he died. Not 'I *will* provide,' mind you, but 'I *have* provided.' And I am sure he has, I feel as sure of it as I do of standing here. There's a will somewhere on earth, and some day it will be found. It may be in this house, or it may not. God alone knows. But he was a man of his word and he would not leave me to the parish in my old age."

She poured out this tirade with breathless fervour, as if it discharged a load from her heart. Peggy was deeply impressed and gazed at her with fascinated eyes.

"You think, then," she said, after a pause, "that by keeping near this house you may discover the will. I hardly see how you expect to do that."

"I don't know how myself, ma'am, but something holds me to Leatheringham and tells me I must not go far from this place.

It may be that a letter may come to me from a lawyer in London. He told me once he'd been seeing a London lawyer. And, do you know, ma'am,—you'll hardly believe it"—she lowered her voice slightly—"his cousin never tried to find that lawyer. He sent his own lawyers down here and I told them Mr. Barker had a legal adviser in London, but they never took no notice. I thought they would have advertised."

"Why didn't you?" Peggy asked.

"It wasn't my business, ma'am, and wouldn't have looked well. But that London lawyer may hear of the death somehow, and write; so I must be here."

"Did you look for the will?"

"High and low, ma'am. Of course his desks and papers were all locked up, and taken away by Mr. Daniel Barker's lawyers when they came down, and of course I gave the keys up at once. But I searched in every corner of the house, even under the carpets and up chimneys—knowing his funny secret ways—but I couldn't find anything."

"I suppose you didn't suspect any foul play on the other Mr. Barker's part? That the will may have been among his papers and concealed or destroyed by him in his own interests?"

The woman paused before replying.

"No, ma'am," she said at last. "He's a man I never liked—and his cousin didn't like him—but I can't believe he could have done anything so wicked as that, though, sometimes, it has come into my mind. No—I won't believe it. He couldn't sleep in his bed of nights if he'd wronged his dead cousin like that. Mr. Barker—my Mr. Barker, would haunt him."

Peggy started at the word "haunt."

"I should think if he haunted anywhere it would be here,"

she suggested, watching the effect of her words. Again Susan Cleaver paused before replying.

"I've thought that," she said, then: "and if I tell you something, ma'am, will you be good enough not to repeat it to a soul? I don't want to be taken to a lunatic asylum."

"Of course I shall respect any confidence of yours," said Peggy, with a creepy feeling in her nerves. What was she going to hear?

In a lowered voice, almost a whisper, Susan Cleaver said: "I *have* seen and heard things in this house when I was alone here; things I couldn't account for nohow, unless it was *him*."

"What sort of things?"

"Oh, the moving about of furniture at night, and the dogs barking like they used to when he went out to them. That was before they were destroyed, ma'am. Beautiful creatures! It was a cruel shame to kill them, young and healthy as they were, and many tears I've shed thinking of them. They were never savage with me, poor things, and could have been tamed with kindness—and freedom."

"It was more cruel to keep them chained than to kill them," said Peggy, who had pronounced ideas on the chaining of dogs and caging of birds.

"I used to tell him so, but he didn't see it. He never seemed able to read other people's feelings, and he couldn't put himself in the dogs' place and know what they felt, as I could."

"When you heard the dogs, and they were then alive, you say, they may have been barking at cats."

"They may, of course. But I know their different barks, when they were pleased or angry. And it wasn't the angry bark I heard, but pleased and joyful, like they used to be when he went to feed them or take them for a run in the grounds. Haven't you ever noticed the difference in a dog's bark, ma'am?"

Peggy had, and said so. She knew something of dogs and had loved one, at least.

"You said that you saw things, too," she went on. "What was it you saw?"

"Shadows—moving shadows. And one night I could have sworn I saw *him*, on the top of the stairs when I went up to bed. It may have been fancy, but it was real enough to make me cry out and run back to the kitchen for a light. I was going without a candle as it was bright moonlight. And another night, when I was hunting about, I saw a face—his face. But it faded out directly."

Peggy gave a little shiver.

"Why didn't he have the electric light put in?" she asked. "It runs past the gate."

"It was one of his odd fancies, ma'am, to have nothing but lamps and candles. He said what was good enough for his father was good enough for him; and he wasn't going to put money into the pockets of any company. You see, he quarrelled with the Gas Company about some shares he thought he ought to have had. He did quarrel with people rather often, being easily annoyed if crossed."

"Did he quarrel with the Electric Company too?"

"No, but he had the idea that electricity was dangerous. 'It's like lightning—you never know where it will have you,' he said, and was always telling me about houses that were burnt down through the wires fusing."

"Queer creature!" mused Peggy.

"He was, ma'am. Very queer and different from other people; but *good.* There never was a better man at heart. He gave a lot away that nobody knew nothing of—especially to children—orphans and cripples and so on. But I am taking up too much of your time, ma'am. I hope you'll forgive me for trespassing on it so long."

"That's all right. I've been very much interested in what you have told me, and if you will leave your address I will certainly let you know if I want any help. Good morning."

When the visitor had gone, Peggy sat thinking for some time. Her mind had been switched back to her old fears and sensations.

"Strange!" she thought. "I felt there was something queer about the house, from the very first. And now she tells me she has seen and heard things here. She doesn't strike me as a nervous and imaginative person either. I wish she hadn't told me. I shall think of it at night and be afraid to go upstairs. Oh, dear! I do hope I shan't see anything. If only we hadn't taken this house! But no one could guess it was haunted, by the look of it."

She did not consider that her promise to the woman bound her to secrecy so far as Percy was concerned. She could never keep anything from him, and he would never repeat what she told him. So, after dinner that night, Peggy launched out into a graphic account of the interview with Susan Cleaver.

CHAPTER IX

PERCY was obviously impressed by the woman's earnest vindication of her late employer, but laughed at her superstitious beliefs. He was also rather annoyed by them, knowing the effect they were likely to have on Peggy's imaginative mind.

"Of course you have too much sense, my Own," he said, "to take any notice of what the poor ignorant creature said about hauntings. She would naturally be prone to strange fancies, being here alone after the old boy died, and in low spirits. It is very decent of her to speak so well of him, when he has treated her so scandalously, but it doesn't do to swallow everything people of that kind say. You must caution her, if ever she does come here charing, not to talk about her experiences in the dark, or we shall soon find ourselves left in the lurch without servants. I hope that isn't her game—to scare them away so that she can take their place here as maid-of-all-work! It wouldn't be a bad wheeze."

"If you saw her, you'd never suspect such a thing," said Peggy indignantly. "She is the last woman in the world to be capable of doing anything so sneaky. But, anyway, it would take more than that to frighten Cookie and Nanny. They are very matter-of-fact and devoted to the children and us."

As it happened the matter was put to the test the very next day; for at the time Mrs. Tubb was to arrive in the morning her little girl came to say she was "took bad" and couldn't come. The visitor being expected next day, it was necessary to have some help in the house, so Peggy went to seek Susan Cleaver, who at once stepped into the breach. She proved herself, as expected, extremely efficient; set to work the moment she crossed the threshold; did not talk, but took hold of things and did as she was told without question. Cookie, like most good servants, had her own "little ways" and liked them to be followed. Susan Cleaver followed her directions implicitly and succeeded in pleasing her, which, as Peggy told Percy at lunch, was "everything." Cookie was busy at her own job, making cakes and pastry and sweets of various kinds. Susan polished and swept and washed briskly, doing as much in an hour as the other woman had done in three. Peggy, who had been worried and flustered at first by the non-appearance of her charwoman, drew breath again with relief and felt no more anxiety lest her new home should not shine in the eyes of her friend.

"That's something like a help," Cook said, when Susan had gone; "she doesn't potter about, asking what she's to do next, like Mrs. Tubb, jabbering all the time. She just takes one thing after another and does it. I wish we could always have her."

"You like her, Cookie?"

"I like anyone as does their work well and is some use," was the reply; "and besides being the right sort, 'm, I'm sorry for the poor thing—treated like what she has been, seemingly. Cruel, I call it."

"You know who she is then, and all about her," said Peggy, somewhat surprised at this speech.

"Oh yes, 'm. Everyone knows about Miss Cleaver, as was Mr. Barker's housekeeper all them years. It's a great come-down for her, to go out a-charing. Nobody ever thought she'd 'ave to get another job after he'd gone, as he'd no chick or child to leave his money to—only a bachelor cousin, older than himself and richer nor he was. He might have left her at least ten shillings a week, after all her faithful service to him—and cutting her off from all her friends, as he did. I don't suppose she's been able to save much out of the low wages he gave her—according to what I've heard."

"Does she talk about it to people?"

"No, 'm. She keeps very quiet about it, they say, being proud and not asking for pity. And she won't hear a word against him. But everyone thinks it's a shame as she was treated so—which it is."

Mrs. Millis arrived the next afternoon and the two friends met with keen pleasure. Joan was a little, plump, dark woman, with laughing eyes, the opposite of Peggy. They had much in common; their babies, their houses, their love of pretty things (including pretty clothes) and of tennis, dancing, theatres, music, and books. They were also alike in their sense of humour and capacity for enjoying all the fun in life. Joan was delighted to hear she was to be taken to the Badminton Club one night; to the theatre another night, to the *Thé Dansant* one afternoon, and another afternoon was to be Peggy's 'Bridge Drive.'

"It's a sort of house-warming," she said, "to which I've asked all the women who have called on me. And I've got lovely prizes—though I say it. You shall see them and choose which you'd like if you win."

How they talked! Peggy had to trot out all her treasures. Her children first, of course, pronounced by Joan to be quite the nicest she had ever seen, next to her own. She had brought them toys and they found her a jolly playmate. After the long visit to the nursery there were other things to see; Peggy's and Joan's new gowns and hats. The bridge prizes, Percy's drawings, the worked pole-screen and other 'antiques.'

Percy was at the top of his form and kept them laughing all through dinner. They were smoking over their coffee in the drawing-room afterwards when there came Nanny to the door and said:

"If you please, 'm, would you mind coming up to Billikin, he won't go to sleep but keeps crying and disturbing Fliss."

Peggy ran upstairs quickly, a trifle worried. She was, like all young mothers, haunted by fears of croup or epidemics. The little "hobgoblin," as they called him was such a healthy and merry baby he could not be crying for nothing.

"He keeps on saying: 'See funny man,' " said Nanny as they went in.

"What is it, my pet?" Peggy asked, bending over the cot in the dim room, where her baby boy sat bolt upright, his little fair head all rumpled and his eyes too bright.

"What does Billy want? Lie down and go to sleep, darling."

She laid her hand on his head as she spoke. It was not hot, but he resisted her effort to make him lie down.

"See funny man," he piped.

"What on earth does he mean?" Peggy asked the nurse.

"I don't know, 'm. But the children are always talking a lot about a funny old man they see in the garden."

"Do they mean Judkins?"

"No, 'm, not Judkins. They know him. They say it's an old man with a beard who sits on the seat round the big tree and smiles at them. I think Gib must have made him up out of his own head, for I haven't seen anybody."

"See funny man," put in Billikin. Peggy felt a little shiver run down her spine.

"No, pet, not to-night. Funny man gone to bye-byes now, where all little boys ought to be. Lie down and Mummie will tell you a lovely story about a bunny rabbit who lived down in a hole with his family and only came up when he wanted a nice meal of lettuce in Daddy's garden."

She soothed and coaxed him to lie down, and, sitting by his bed, told a rambling story in a low, monotonous voice, which soon had the desired effect. But she felt very cold when she got up to steal from the room, and very nervous, for there was no light save from the moonlit windows and Nanny had gone downstairs again. Out on the landing, where a small lamp burned, she could have sworn she saw a strange shape on the wall, and her own shadow, as she passed the lamp, made her start and shudder. A voice from the bigger children's room, leading out from their own, arrested her.

"Nanny."

"Is that you, Gib? Why aren't you asleep?" she asked, looking in.

"I heard Billy calling. What does he want, Mummie?"

"Ssh! He's asking for a funny man. I don't know what he means."

"I do," said Gib, sleepily. "It's the one we see in the garden."

"What's he like, Gib?"

"He has a beard and he laughs at us. Who is he, mum, do you think?"

Peggy did not reply, but asked:

"Has he spoken to you, or touched you?"

"No, Mummie; he never speaks, and when we go up to him he goes away."

"Where does he go?"

"I dunno. Behind the tree, or somewhere."

"I must find out who it is," said Peggy, speaking as naturally as she could. "And now, go to sleep or you'll disturb K. See, she's moving. Good night, darling."

"Good ni'," murmured Gib, and she went downstairs.

"What was the matter?" Percy asked, as she came into the room again.

"Oh, the usual thing," she answered. "The children have been indulging in their imaginations."

"What is it this time?" said Percy. The irony of her tone was not lost on him. "Dogs again?"

"No, an old man with a beard, who sits on the seat round the beech and laughs at them, but he goes behind the tree—or somewhere—when they try to get near him."

"Who told you that stuff?" queried Percy, contemptuously.

"First Nanny. Billikin kept crying out for the 'funny man,' and she told me the children had seen one in the garden. Then Gib called to me and I asked about him."

"Gib is his mother's own son, full of fancy and invention," said Percy, laughing. "I wonder what he'll think of next. The other day he told me, quite seriously, that he had a beautiful black horse in the stable and was going to ride to York on it. I had been relating Dick Turpin's ride to him."

"Children's imaginations are very wonderful," observed Joan. "They can make themselves believe anything they like to believe. You remember Stevenson's essay about them? Marvellously true. There's a very thin veil between the real and unreal with them, and that's why we so often think they're lying when the darlings make things up and repeat them. They *think* they're true, I've no doubt. At least that seems to be R. L. S.'s idea."

"One can imagine the things *he* made up when he was a child," Percy chuckled; "and how he shocked his dear Scotch mamma with them."

"My little Winsome is a rare hand at pretending," said Joan; "I think she'd run your Gilbert very close, Peggy. The other day——"

One story led to another, and Joan enjoyed herself talking of her children and their richly inventive capacities. Percy occasionally chipped in with a story about Gib and Fliss, and the two laughed together. But Peggy did not laugh. She sat with her feet on the fender knitting a little sock and thinking hard. It didn't matter what Perks said (her underlip was firmly set against the upper), he could laugh at her and chaff her as much as he pleased, but *she* knew when Gib was making up things, if Perks didn't, and she knew the child had spoken the truth to-night. Besides, there was the evidence of Billikin. Was it likely that a two-year-old would keep on about the "funny man," if he hadn't seen anything? In some instances, she decided, it is more absurd to disbelieve than to believe. You have to invent reasons for your disbelief that do not hold water.

She remembered how, after seeing a famous thought-reader perform at the Hippodrome in London, Perks, who had not been present, tried to laugh her out of believing the evidence of her own senses by suggesting confederates. The thought-reader had read correctly visiting cards, numbers on cheques, names in watches and hats, read by her collaborators in the stalls, dress circle, upper circle and gallery, in all making a dozen or so of tests. And Percy tried to persuade her that every person who offered a card or a watch or a cheque was a confederate! He could not see the absurdity of this—the expense, the danger of betrayal—the ease with which such trickery could be exposed; or explain how every innocent person offering a test could be ignored. It had seemed to Peggy, then, that the sceptic can swallow more improbabilities than the humbly receptive believer. And she thought this now. She thought it was simply ridiculous to credit little Gib not only with inventing a bearded man in the garden, but with imposing his invention on the other two children. There was no further doubt in her mind. Those babes of hers were clairvoyant and could see what others could not see. Was the same strange gift hers, and had she really seen the figure leaning over their garden gate that Percy declared to be the shadow of a fir tree? She devoutly hoped not.

CHAPTER X

PROGRESSIVE bridge is a great game and very popular in country towns, where social parties take, to some extent, the place of theatres. It is particularly delectable to hostesses, as more than half the fun lies in preparing for the function; laying in stocks of dainty cakes for tea, delicious sweets for the bonbon dishes on each table, and, above all, in choosing the prizes. Sometimes, of course, the "Drive" (as it is generally and affectionately termed) is given at night, when the feminine element is leavened by the masculine, and refreshments are slightly varied; but as a rule progressive bridge (or whist) is an afternoon affair, starting any time after three and lasting till it is time to go home and dress for dinner.

Peggy and Joan enjoyed themselves thoroughly getting ready for the Drive. Peggy had hired a number of small tables and on each of these a number had to be pinned, beside which were placed two packs of new cards and a *bonbonnière* full of chocolates and fondants. Flowers were arranged in every available corner, and candles to eke out the light of lamps, which would have to be used after tea, if not before. The lighting up of the room was Peggy's chief concern, as a lamp, delightful in its close proximity, does not give far-reaching rays. It would be difficult to get enough light for each table, she was aware, and to arrange lamps and candles so as to illuminate the darker corners required some thinking out. Then there were the tea-tables to set in the dining-room. Peggy had engaged Susan Cleaver to help, and she was a host in herself, working deftly and quietly, shifting chairs and tables, making sensible suggestions, running errands for things forgotten, or not sent in good time by the tradespeople. Early in the day Percy showed a disposition to hover about them, getting in their way and criticising everything they did, after the futile manner of men generally when they attempt to interfere in women's business; but he was so promptly snubbed by Peggy and Joan that he took himself off, with a chuckle, to his den and remained there till lunch time.

Flushed with excitement and looking deliciously pretty, in a jade-green *crêpe de Chine* frock, Peggy received her guests soon after three o'clock, welcoming them as if they had been old friends and introducing each one to Joan as they entered. It must be confessed that she mixed up their names a bit and was not quite sure, all the afternoon, which was Mrs. Conyers Jones and which Mrs. Markham Smith; they were so much alike, and, to make matters worse, wore similar hats. But she did not betray her doubts and glided over her difficulty in introduction by saying: "My old friend, Mrs. Millis" and omitting the other name.

Peggy was very happy when she saw the whole party seated and the first game begun. She had had the usual disappointments at the eleventh hour, when two excuses were sent in—one lady ill, and one kept at home by a sick child; but by playing herself and making Percy play, the gaps were filled. She had not intended to play, but really enjoyed doing so, and she felt that everything was going smoothly. Her frock she knew was a success and suited her. Percy told her, when she came down, that she looked "a perfect peach"; the lamp and candle-light was becoming, the chatter was gay and all the women seemed to be enjoying themselves. Peggy loved entertaining, as most highly vitalized and warm-hearted people do. She was proud of her well-arranged house and good-looking, famous husband (for she regarded him as famous), and she was even more proud of her four lovely children, who were brought in during tea-time, clothed in delicate raiment, to receive the compliments of her guests.

The children were not hampered by shyness. Fliss promptly laid a tiny finger on a mole decorating Mrs. Gordon Green's chin and asked: "What's that?" while Billikin reiterated "Want cake" many times rapidly till he was given a piece. Gib asked Mrs. Gayworthy politely if he might have her vanity bag to keep, as it would do so nicely to collect caterpillars in, and would she like to see his caterpillar cage? K. called attention to her new frock and vouchsafed the information that her new knickers had real lace on them, which she promptly exhibited. Thus the young fry amused Peggy's guests until Gib jogged one of their elbows and sent a cup of tea in the lap of a silk gown, upon which all four were dismissed to the nursery and their mother felt the first jar to her elation of spirits.

The first, but by no means the last. For the rest of her day was a series of shocks and terrors.

While her guests were still chattering over tea and cigarettes in the dining-room, she went into the drawing-room to light up, for it was now quite dark. She had lighted the lamps and had started on the candles when a curious sound made her pause. She listened. There was a gentle knocking, as of a man tapping his pipe out on the wall near which she stood. Her breath stopped, then began to come fast. She pulled herself together and crossed the room to the candles on the piano. Again the raps came, now they were on this side of the wall. She almost dropped the taper she was holding in the sudden tremor that shot through her frame, and could not hold it steadily to the candle wicks. Her heart began to thump so violently that it almost drowned the knocking, which, however, persisted. Then she held her breath a moment to listen.

The soft, eerie light threw strange shadows about the room. She saw the drawn curtains by the bow-window move and had much ado to suppress a shriek. Then she pulled herself together. How silly! when she had opened the window herself, to air the room. Of course, the wind was blowing the curtains.

Crossing the room to close the lower window, she looked out into the darkness, now deepened by the light within the room. And, facing her in the gloom outside, was—*something!* The figure of a man, shadowy, barely defined. With a gasp she shut the window quickly and drew the curtains over it. Fool! Her own reflection, of course, thrown by the light behind her. But she felt suddenly faint with apprehension. You can't argue against such fear.

But she managed to light the rest of the candles and walk back to the other room, where the talk and laughter revived her and she said: "All ready. Shall we go in?"

As they trooped back to the card tables, Joan seized her arm.

"What is the matter, Peg? Are you all right? You look so white."

"Nonsense," she laughed nervously. "Of course I'm all right."

And, as she spoke, her colour came back to her face, reassuring Joan, who had been really alarmed at its death-like pallor.

Everyone admired the effect of the lamp and candle-light, to which so few people are now accustomed. "Charming! . . . Such a lovely change after the crude electric light . . . so becoming to the complexion . . . doesn't show up one's wrinkles," and so on, the gentle ladies cooed; while they privately commiserated poor Mrs. Dacre for having no electricity or gas in her house, and wished they could see their cards a little better!

It was after the second round that Peggy heard the knocking again. She had assured herself, in the meantime, that it must have been done by Judkins, hammering up a climber on the wall, but he left at five o'clock and it was quite half-past now. Besides, he would not be hammering up a creeper in the dark. And, this time, she heard it on the inner wall; the one between the room and the hall.

"Do you hear anything?" she asked the three women at her table, pausing in her play—"a kind of—knocking?"

"A knocking! No. Do you?"

It was a quiet moment, in the middle of a game. She heard the rapping again, distinctly.

"I thought I heard something," she faltered, "but if you don't, I suppose . . . "

"I can't hear anything, can you, Dorothy?" one said to another.

None of them had heard anything.

But the whole room heard a little shriek afterwards, as Peggy deliberately threw away her last valuable trump on her partner's trick.

"Oh, I am *so* sorry!" she cried abjectly. "I didn't see . . . I was thinking of something else. Do forgive me, partner."

The game went on. The knocking ceased on the wall, but seemed to continue in Peggy's head. She could not keep her attention on the cards. The climax came when she changed tables and, glancing across the room, her eye was caught by the pole-screen standing by the fire-place in a shadowy corner.

There appeared the perfect outline of a face in it!

The subject of the tapestry on one side of the screen was the usual eighteenth-century pastoral; a shepherdess leaning on a crook, with a badly deformed lamb at her feet, and a shepherd leaning over a gate behind; on the other side was a group of flowers. Peggy loved the picture and valued the screen as something deliciously quaint and fascinating. It was with an incredible sensation of shock that she saw, or thought she saw, the old-world scene change to a man's bearded face. Her gaze was caught and riveted, in a look of frozen horror. She could not shift her eyes from it, and, naturally, the three other players at her table turned to look too.

"What is the matter, Mrs. Dacre?" asked one, alarmed by her expression and the sudden ghastly paleness of her face.

The words brought her quickly to her normal poise. Indeed, the impression had been but momentary; the face had appeared and faded out in a few seconds. With a laughing apology and a feeble excuse, she seized up the cards to shuffle and went on playing; but her hands were moist and trembling, her lips dry and her heart gave queer little jumps. She played badly again and, it is to be feared, badly damaged her reputation as a bridge expert that afternoon.

When the games were all over, the prizes presented and accepted, with immense appreciation of their quality, and the guests began to depart, Peggy recovered her lost spirits and was happy again. Her enjoyment had been spoilt by what she had seen and heard, but the admiration and gratitude of the prize-winners, the assurance of all her guests that they had spent a most delightful afternoon, restored her natural buoyancy and she attributed all her qualms to her own foolish imagination. Of course she hadn't heard or seen anything uncanny, really. Everything could be quite normally accounted for, she felt sure. The knocking had come from the kitchen or nursery; the form and face she had seen were due to candle-light and shadows. She joined Joan and Percy in a cocktail and a cigarette, thankful to sit down and enjoy these luxuries, for she had not been able to get much tea, being too much engaged in looking after her guests, and she was tired with the effort of entertaining.

But she was restless, and, while Percy and Joan were talking in the morning-room, she went back to the drawing-room, to put out the candles and pack up the cards. There she found Susan Cleaver, with her back to the door, staring, it seemed, at the pole-screen. She turned, with a start, as Peggy entered.

CHAPTER XI

"EXCUSE me, ma'am, but I am so glad you have this screen and that it did not go out of the house," she said; "Mr. Barker was very proud of it and he was always telling me how valuable it was, and how he picked it up cheap. Only a week before he was taken ill he told me I was to have it after he was dead, but he didn't think he was going to die so soon—no more did I."

"If he gave it to you, why didn't you take it?"

"He didn't *give* it to me, ma'am. He only said I was to have it—'it will be yours some day' was how he put it, and I thought he'd left it to me in his will. Of course I couldn't take it, and I didn't like to say anything about it. Shall I begin to put the room straight now, ma'am? That's what I came in for."

"Yes, do. I was just going to put out the candles and collect the cards." She paused, and went on: "You have been most helpful to-day, Miss Cleaver, and I don't know what I should have done without you. I am really surprised at your capability considering the quiet life you must have led here for so many years."

"You are very good to say so, ma'am, I'm sure," the woman replied, her face lighting up with pleasure. "I did feel a little awkward and out of practice at first; but I was a parlour-maid once, and haven't forgotten how to wait at table and so on. Of course there wasn't much to do in that line for Mr. Barker, but when you've once learnt how to do things properly you don't forget them, I think."

"It's a skilled job, no doubt," said Peggy, smiling. "I expect you had a good deal of experience of it in your youth."

"I had, ma'am, and in good houses. But my mother taught me first. She was servant in a big house for many years before she became housekeeper and married the butler. It was only the cooking that bothered me, when I came to Mr. Barker's. But I soon learned to cook, and what he liked. And there was never any company; only him."

"I wonder what he would have said to this party in his house!" Peggy exclaimed.

Susan Cleaver threw up her hands.

"He would have hated it." Then she added, with a curious expression on her face: "He *did* hate it."

"What do you mean, Miss Cleaver?" asked Peggy, puzzled both by her words and the queer glint in her eyes.

"Oh, nothing, ma'am. Only I always feel that he isn't very far away. I did to-day. It is silly of me, no doubt, but I can't help it."

Peggy, who had extinguished some of the candles while Susan did the others, and was packing up cards, paused and, facing the woman, asked the question that refused to be held back:

"Did you hear anything this afternoon?"

"Yes, ma'am, I did—several times."

"A knocking?"

The woman nodded and drew closer to Peggy. "And I *saw* something, too—outside," she whispered.

"So did I."

It was out. Peggy was instantly angry with herself. Now the story would spread of a haunted house. Susan Cleaver would probably tell the maids, and other people. Percy would be annoyed.

"Of course it was only fancy," she hastened to add. "It would never do to let such a silly tale get about. We must keep our superstitious fancies to ourselves, Miss Cleaver."

"I should never dream of saying anything about it to anyone, ma'am. I shouldn't have mentioned it to you, if you hadn't asked me. People would only think me mad and want to lock me up in an asylum! So you heard the knocking too, and saw him in the garden. Oh dear! The poor old gentleman—how unhappy he must be! And we can't do anything to help him."

This sudden and definite lament for the restless spirit she believed to be haunting the house gave Peggy a curious sensation. The whole matter, from being nebulous and within the bounds of nervous fancy, suddenly crystallized into something appallingly real and incontrovertible. One may reason away one's own visions, but when they are seen and definitely affirmed by another person, it is not so easy to dispose of them as 'unsubstantial fabric.'

But there was no time for further conversation, as Joan and Percy came into the room at this moment and sat down by the fire to talk, having let the fire in the other room go out. Percy's comments on the party and the guests sent Joan into little gusts of laughter.

"The lady with half a rooster on her head hadn't much idea of the game," he observed. "She thought it dreadful to lead a king before the ace was out. Nothing, she observed, would induce her to make such a treasonable sacrifice of royalty. She would rather go to bed with his majesty,—or to that effect."

"Well, you don't usually——" Joan began.

"I admit it isn't common," Percy chipped into the pause: "But then kings are not very common."

"I mean one doesn't lead kings before the aces are out."

"Oh, doesn't one? You may not. Some of us have been taught to lead the highest of our partner's suit."

"Of course. I didn't think of that."

"There was another 'fair female, unadorned and plain'[7]—plainer than usual, in fact,—who punished your chocolate creams rather severely, Peg. I never glanced her way but I caught one travelling to her capacious maw."

"I hope you didn't look her way too often, Perks."

"Not oftener than I could avoid, I assure you, although she certainly 'shone forth solicitous to bless in all the glaring impotence of dress.' What did you think of the beehive that crowned her noble brow, Joan? Wasn't that bow at the top topping?"

"I don't know which you mean. Was it the lady in an orange and red striped jumper?"

"Yes. Didn't she remind you of a jazz band?"

"I thought her quite a jolly woman."

"Oh, she was, undoubtedly. But isn't a jazz band jolly enough for you? I wish certain colours didn't make me feel sea-sick! Now I liked the little grey lady with a penthouse roof on. Her eyes were like round windows under a thatch. Why do women try to hide their eyebrows? Are they out of fashion? What was the name of the sweet thing in blue bombazine, Peg?"

"I didn't see anybody in blue bombazine."

"Life of my Soul, you did; and gave her a prize for being a booby. I wish some one would give me a prize for the same reason."

"The dress was jade, not blue, Perks—jade morocain—awfully pretty, I thought, and well cut."

"Only a jade would ever think of wearing jade. That accounts for her looking so jaded, poor nymph! Not that she made no effort to restore with art her fading charms. I caught her at it more

---

[7] From Oliver Goldsmith's poem 'The Deserted Village', as is Percy's next quotation beginning 'shone forth solicitous to bless'.

than once. In fact—I'll tell you a secret, Joan—one you would never guess. What do you think they carry about in those cunning little bags? I imagined they were only to hold trifles that could be picked up—in the way of chocolates, etc. But no. They contain certain restoratives to the complexion and little mirrors. I watched their owners when they weren't munching or playing cards."

"Clever boy! How observant you are!"

"One can't live with a prodigy like my Pegtop without becoming keen as a razor. She intrigues one's mind continually. Don't you, my Blessing."

"What did you say, Perks?" she asked.

"Wool-gathering, poor dear," observed her husband, *sotto voce* to Joan, and tapping his forehead significantly. "She is often taken like that. The thing is not to notice it." Then to Peggy he said blandly:

"I was merely remarking, my Heart's Treasure, that your party has been a great success. I enjoyed it."

"Glad to hear it," she smiled.

"I enjoyed it immensely. It was as good as a dog show, and almost as quiet. No doubt you have acquired much merit in this small community. It was, perhaps, a trifle unfortunate that the fan prize fell to a fat and fifty dame whose dancing days are probably over. But she may have a daughter."

"People use fans at theatres," observed Joan.

"So they do, madam. Why are you always right? By the way, Pegotty, are we going to be fed any more to-night, or is the feast of reason and flow of soul we have enjoyed, combined with tea, cakes, and chocolates, considered sufficient for our carnal appetites?"

"Dinner won't be long. What a hungry pig you are!"

"So would you be if you'd been waiting on a ravenous horde

of women all tea-time and exerting every nerve to make yourself agreeable to 'em."

"Which I did do."

"Yes, but with you agreeability has become a habit and requires no effort. In my case it is entirely different. I am exhausted. I am faint for want of nourishment. And if you think I'm going to change to-night, my Bright Particular Star, you are jolly well mistaken."

"Nobody axed you," said Peggy; "on such occasions as this we can't be bothered. Are you starving too, Joan?"

"Not I. Didn't you see me at tea?"

"I did," exclaimed Percy. "Those éclairs! No wonder I couldn't find a crumb of anything when you'd gone and I went round to clear the dishes."

Joan promptly threw a cushion at him. It missed him and lighted on the pole-screen, which it brought clattering to the floor."

Peggy shrieked. "Oh, Joan, how could you be so careless? You might have broken the glass."

As she picked it up and set it on its feet again Peggy could have sworn she felt a nervous contraction of the muscles, and recalled the face she had seen in the screen. Or was it that the recollection made her nerves quiver? There is no saying. She did not dare, however, to glance at the worked picture as she set it by the wall.

At that moment the gong sounded and they went in to dinner.

CHAPTER XII

WHEN they went up to bed that night Peggy stayed, as usual, in her friend's room for a last chat by the fire. They talked over the party and the guests for some time, and then Peggy asked abruptly:

"Did you . . . I suppose you didn't hear anything while we were playing this afternoon?"

"Hear anything? What kind of thing? I heard a great buzz of talk."

"I mean—a knocking."

Joan thought a moment. Then she said:

"Yes I did—now you speak of it. I wondered what it was. On the wall."

Peggy shivered in the warm room. It was not the answer she expected, or hoped for. She wanted a negative that would have proved her own fears fanciful.

"What did you think it could be?" she asked.

"Oh, I suppose it was the children overhead. The day nursery is over the drawing-room, isn't it?"

"But it sounded on the wall, as you said."

"I know; but sounds are difficult to locate sometimes."

"To me," said Peggy, "it sounded like some one hammering nails into the wall and I thought it might be Judkins nailing up a creeper. But when it came again, I knew it wasn't he. What could it have been?"

"To tell the truth, Peg, I was so intent on the game, and everyone was talking so fast, I didn't notice the knocking very much, and shouldn't have thought any more about it if you hadn't asked me. But no doubt it can be easily accounted for."

"Susan Cleaver heard it too."

"It must have been the children. They adore making noise, as you know."

Peggy reflected. Could it have been the children after all?

"What did you think it was—the ghost?" queried Joan, laughing.

Peggy had told her about the strange happenings in the house, and Joan had been impressed. But she could not resist teasing Peggy.

"You wouldn't laugh, Jo, if you had heard and seen the things I have," said Peggy earnestly, and she went on to tell her of the shadowy form she had seen outside in the garden, and the face in the screen; concluding:

"You may think I am mad, if you like, but I am certainly convinced that this house is haunted. And there is every reason why it should be haunted."

"Because the old man died without a will!" scoffed Joan.

"Because he broke a promise and committed an act of injustice," replied Peggy, in a low voice. "If any unhappy spirits are ever permitted to return and attempt to right a wrong they have done, I believe that poor soul might be."

As the two women sat staring into the fire a sound they both heard swept through the room. It was like a gusty sigh. Instinctively each of them took a hasty glance over her shoulder.

"Oh, don't!" exclaimed Joan. "You give me the creeps, Peg, and my nerves are all tingling. I thought I heard something then."

"The sound of a sigh," whispered Peggy.

Joan did not reply.

"Don't you believe that such things do happen sometimes?"

Peggy went on, "or do you think all stories about *revenants* and the reports we constantly read of in the papers about haunted houses are all lies—mere sensational fiction?"

"I don't know," said Joan, hesitatingly, "I've never quite been able to decide. Some of the experiences I have heard first-hand have certainly shaken my scepticism a good deal. I could tell you some instances——"

She broke off. "But not now, my dear. The atmosphere is too eerie already and I have to sleep alone, remember, without a nice substantial husband between me and the unseen world, as you have. I should think good old matter-of-fact Percy would ward off any ghost. Think of me alone, in this haunted bed-chamber! I declare I'm all goose-flesh. I hope this wasn't the Old Man's room."

"No, I believe we have it. But if you don't believe in ghosts you can't be frightened of them."

"That's where you make a mistake, my dear. Belief has nothing to do with reasoning. I may reason the whole thing away in my mind as absurd, but I can't reason with my nerves. I shall probably have the jumps all night."

"Then I'll stay and sleep with you."

"You will not. I shouldn't dream of letting you. What would Percy think of me? I don't want to forfeit his esteem for ever. Good night, darling, sleep well. We must make up our minds not to see or hear anything, and then we shall not. *Bonne nuit.*"

She bustled Peggy out of the room with these words and proceeded with her final preparations for the night, humming softly to herself as she did so. Before getting into bed she made up the fire. It was cheery company and threw its flickering light about the room.

Peggy got to bed quickly and snuggled under the clothes, longing for Percy to come up. He came presently and, thinking her asleep, moved softly about the room. Once in bed he was soon in a sound sleep, and Peggy was getting drowsy when a sound at her door made her wide awake in an instant.

The skin of her head seemed to tighten, as she listened.

"Peg! Are you asleep?" came in a faint voice from outside.

She drew a deep breath of relief and sprang to the door.

"Joan! What is it?"

"I can't sleep," Joan whispered, "I keep thinking I hear . . . . things. It's awfully silly, I know, but if you *could* come—if Percy——"

"He's sound asleep; of course I'll come."

She snatched up her dressing-gown, slipped her feet into pretty bedroom moccasins and went out, closing the door behind her very softly. The two shivering women crept across the landing silently and got into the large bed without a word. The fire was nearly out, but the room was not cold enough to account for the nervous shivers that went through them both, as they huddled down and listened, tense and almost breathless, until, after some time thus, first one and then the other dropped off to sleep.

. . . . .

Suddenly Peggy woke up, startled and shaking. A sound as of some one shifting heavy furniture about overhead was in her ears, and then, suddenly there came a distinct bump on the ceiling.

Now the room over the guest-chamber was a low attic in the roof, used for boxes and other lumber. She listened a few moments, petrified with fright, the skin of her head tingling, and her heart thumping so loudly that it began to drown all other noise.

"Joan!" she managed to gasp at last, grasping her friend's arm and shaking her ruthlessly: "Wake up, Joan. Do you hear that?"

Even as she spoke, compunction seized her at the thought of her own selfishness. Why should she terrify her guest because she was terrified herself? But panic is the slave of impulse. She had not paused to think.

"Wh . . . what is it?" Joan muttered, rousing herself. "What . . . oh, Peggy—it's you."—for the moment she seemed surprised to find Peggy near her. "Is anything the matter?"

"No—I'm so sorry to wake you, Joan, but I . . . there are such queer noises overhead." Peggy whispered, and her whisper was blood-curdling. "Listen!"

They both listened intently. For some minutes there was no sound. Then came a sudden bump and the two friends clutched each other convulsively.

"Did you hear it?" gasped Peggy.

"Of course I did. Oh, Peg! There must be some one up there."

"If there is . . . it's the Old Man. It couldn't be anyone else."

"It might be rats."

Peggy ignored this suggestion.

"Whatever it is, it is coming downstairs." she exclaimed: "I heard them creak. Oh, Joan, if it comes here I shall go out of my mind!"

She was shaking all over, as if with ague.[8]

They could hear nothing now, for they both got under the bed-clothes and suffocated there for some time in silence. By degrees their fears diminished and they allowed themselves breathing space. All was quiet again and Joan was dropping off to sleep when Peggy startled her again with another blood-curdling whisper.

"Hark!"

---

[8] Ague: a fever accompanied by chills and shaking.

Joan harkened but could hear nothing.

"The dogs!" breathed Peggy. "Don't you hear them, Joan? It's bad enough"—she began to laugh hysterically—"to be haunted by a human being, but when animals start, it really is thc limit!"

"I can't hear anything," said Joan. "You're strung up, Peg, and must have imagined it."

Even as she spoke, Joan thought she heard the faint bark of a dog, but she made up her mind not to say so. Her task now was to soothe and reassure Peggy, who was over-excited and becoming hysterical.

"I didn't imagine it. They woke me up," declared Peggy. "Oh, I do hope they haven't waked the children."

"Nonsense," said Joan, firmly. "Don't give in to your nerves, Peg. There's no barking. You dreamt it. And if there is—if the Old Man's ghost is hovering about, what harm can it do anyone?"

"It's all very well for you," said Peggy. "You don't have to live in a haunted house. I wish from my heart we'd never heard of the beastly place. I felt there was something wrong with it the moment I got inside."

"Well, if there is, you can get some one to find out the cause. The Society for Psychical Research would doubtless send some one to investigate. Or you could do as a Roman Catholic friend of mine did, have the house exorcised by a priest. There's a form of exorcism, you know, that's been used ever since the Middle Ages against witchcraft and all that sort of thing. My friend was always having queer things happen in his house—heavy pictures and furniture falling down and missing him by an inch; terrible noises at night waking the whole household; illness after illness occurring, till he became convinced there were devils at work."

"Devils! Worse and worse!" groaned Peggy.

"Somewhat *de trop*, I admit, in any good Christian's home," replied Joan, "but you'll be glad to hear the priest was one too many for them. After he had prayed in every room, and sprinkled with holy water and pronounced the Church's blessing, nothing more ever happened. At least, so my friend assured me."

Joan, now thoroughly roused and awake, talked on glibly and quite loudly, hoping to drown any other sound there might be to Peggy's supersensitive ears. And not without effect. Her friend calmed down and the only remark she made at the end of this tirade was:

"You make light of all this, Joan, but in your heart you are not sceptical. Or why were you so scared as to fetch me out of bed to sleep with you?"

"Because I was an ass, my dear, a prey to nerves and suggestion. I was scared. You must remember that I am not accustomed to the deadly stillness of night in the country, and the least sound is magnified. After what you had said about your ghostly noises it was very natural I should fancy I heard strange noises."

"You heard that bump upstairs."

"It was probably my own heart! You frightened me."

"Don't pretend, Joan. I know you're only trying to chaff me out of my fears, but you believe in such things as much as I do, or you wouldn't have heard noises and come to me."

"Well, I suppose I do believe in ghosts—at least, one half of me does, the enquiring half. It's probably a complex—a survival from the past that lies dormant in all of us. But, anyhow, I've heard too many stories of haunted houses, first-hand, to deny positively that they are all mythical. Indeed, I've experienced a manifestation of the kind. There's a house I stay at, in Scotland—you know—the Gillespie's—where it is quite a common event to have one's bedroom door open suddenly in the night and feel one's bed-clothes being pulled off by unseen agency. The Gillespies are so used to it that they don't worry about it at all. They simply get up, shut the door and pull the sheets and blankets over them again. Occasionally a servant hears or sees something uncanny, but, of course, they are not put into any of the haunted rooms and, unless they are told of the ghost, are not troubled."

"You said you had had the experience?"

"Yes; once when I was staying there my door opened in the night, and as there was no wind, and no sound at all, I concluded it was the ghost. I shouldn't have been put into that room only the house was full, and they trusted to luck. These manifestations only occur at intervals, I believe. When I heard the door open I didn't know about the haunting. It came out at breakfast, when I told Mary. They all laughed and I guessed there was something; so I made them tell me. A friend of theirs in the Highlands heard the Headless Horseman of the Maclaines gallop by the house distinctly when he was attending the death-bed of one of the Clan. He was not a man to fancy things, or indulge in fiction; quite a matter-of-fact old boy. But I can tell you something even more amazing than that, if you remind me to-morrow. I think we've had enough of spooks to-night."

"So do I!" declared Peggy: "enough and to spare! We must try to go to sleep. Heavens!"—she looked at her wrist-watch—"if it isn't three o'clock."

"Cock-crow time," exclaimed Joan. "We shan't hear or see anything more of the uncanny, Peg. No self-respecting ghost ever permits himself to be seen or heard after cock-crow, don't you know?"

They were both soon asleep.

CHAPTER XIII

PERCY was very merry at their expense next day. He awoke in the night, he declared, to hear strange whispering and rustling, to find that it all came from a ghost who had evidently slid through the solid door of his room. All he saw was a flutter of white, and when he leant over to poke Peggy in the back—lo! no Peggy was there. The ghost had spirited her off! He professed to have thrust his head under the clothes, shivering with fright.

"What was it *you* saw, Mrs. Joan?" he asked. "Did it wear a white sheet and gibber, or carry its head under its arm? Tell me all about it, that I may sympathise."

"It was a norful sight," responded Joan, playing up to him and rolling her eyes; "enough to frighten anyone, wasn't it, Peg? All in a white glare, with fiery eyes, clanking chains, and grisly moans—a regular Scrooge!"

"What did it come for?" Percy enquired, pleasantly.

"Merely for company," Joan replied, promptly. "It was just lonesome, poor thing, and said 'it's no use going to the man over the way, who is a mere clod, sleeping like a pig, so I've come to you.' "

"Now I wonder who that clod could be," said Percy, reflectively. "Next time you want to borrow my wife, Joan, I wish you'd let me know in advance. These little nocturnal surprises are bad for the artistic temperament."

"I'm not going to borrow her again," Joan declared. "She's worse than a ghost and won't let me sleep. To-night I entertain the Ghostly Visitant alone."

Peggy was silent through all this bandinage, with a vacant smile on her lips. Now she said:

"Cookie and Nannie both heard noises in the night."

"After you suggested it, no doubt," said Percy.

"No, Percy, before. Cookie asked me if I'd heard anything and said she thought there was some one in the attic, next to her room."

"Wonderful imagination, that Cook has!"

"And so has your youngest son," retorted Peggy quickly, "for he woke Nannie crying, and when she asked him what was the matter he said 'naughty bow-wows.' She heard the dogs bark quite plainly, she says."

"Loudly?" asked Joan, blenching a little and thinking of her resolve to sleep alone.

"No, rather faintly, but quite distinct."

"Did she think it sounded like dog spooks?" queried Percy, "and if so, why 'faint'? Wouldn't they be close by, in the yard?"

"I can only tell you what she said, Perks. I can't account for it."

"She is a silly wench," he remarked, "and should not be encouraged. There are dogs barking in yards all over the country—accursed be they!—And it's nothing very astonishing to hear them from all quarters. A heavy bark can be heard for half a mile, or further, when the wind's right for it. Why not cultivate a little horse sense, Peg, and exercise it on your domestics? If you don't take care we shall lose our precious 'stipendiary aids.' No servant ever stops in a haunted house."

But no amount of chaff or scorn could shake Peggy's convictions, founded, as she declared to Joan after breakfast, on the evidence of her senses.

"If you're not going to trust your ears and eyes," she said, "I don't see what you *can* trust. It's easy enough to be sceptical when you're not psychic, like Percy, and nothing from the unseen world gets through to you. But when you hear unaccountable sounds in the dead of night, and see things, as I saw yesterday, to call it mere fancy is simply silly; jumping to an unjustifiable conclusion. It often seems to me, Joan, that sceptics of the supernatural are extraordinarily credulous in their own beliefs. They will accept the flimsiest explanation of the unaccountable rather than own that there may be something our present knowledge cannot explain. Perks, for instance, would believe that a thought-reader could afford to pay confederates to deceive the public all over a huge theatre rather than admit that thought-transference is possible. He would argue that those confederates could command the situation and keep the general public from discovering their complicity. That is what I call credulous."

"It certainly is. Surely everyone, to-day, is coming to see that it isn't safe to deny any possibility, or say anything is unscientific. What has become of the sceptics who laughed at the idea of the world being round? And would anyone, half a century ago, have believed in wireless telegraphy?"

"Of course not. I don't suppose we should, you or I. And certainly Perks wouldn't. To my mind thought-transference is not one whit more wonderful than broadcasting. That is a miracle, of you like!"

"I often wonder how far we shall get in the next ten years," said Joan. "Isn't it rather terrifying to think we may be able to read each other's thoughts?"

"Appalling!"

They both laughed. Then Peggy said:

"What about that ghost story you were to tell me to-day?"

"It isn't a ghost story, proper. It's a story of what is called a 'phantasm of the living.' There's a lot about it in Myers' *Human Personality.*[9] But this case happened to a friend of mine, Emily Carr—you've met her."

"Oh yes. I remember her—an artist."

"When I say it happened to her, that is not quite accurate. Her connection with the affair was accidental, and very extraordinary, I think. But I will tell you her story. She is not fanciful or credulous—or inclined to romance."

"About a year ago she received a commission from a lady in Suffolk, to go down there and paint a miniature from a photograph. It was arranged that she should stay a few days, as the family did not wish the photograph to go out of their hands. It was the only one they had of their mother, who had recently died. Emily went and found them charming; two sisters and a brother. While she was there she happened to mention that she had been staying in Scotland some years before, at a shooting lodge, whose name I have forgotten—let us call it"—she paused—"Oban Lodge."

"As soon as she had spoken this name, her clients exclaimed: 'Oban Lodge! You've stayed there? Then you know about the ghost?' Emily said she did, and observed, laughingly, that it had opened her door one night, and the family had told her all about a little old lady with grey curls who walked round the house at

---

[9] Frederic W. H. Myers was one of the founders of the Society for Psychical Research. His significant work *Human Personality and its Survival of Bodily Death*, published in 1903, presents an overview of his research into the unconscious mind, the nature of human personality, and the possibility of the continued existence of human consciousness after death of the physical body. It also proposes a theory that explains ghost-seeing as the result of telepathy and the projection of a 'phantasm' (whether by a living person or a dead one).

night and occasionally opened their bedroom doors. 'We are quite fond of her,' they said, 'and no one minds her in the least. She has been haunting us for many years now.' "

"The girls laughed and one said: 'You may be surprised to hear that you are painting the portrait of that very ghost! My dear mother used, for years, to have a dream in which she visited a house up in the north that she came to know well. Whenever she dreamt about it she used to tell us in the morning, and describe it minutely. We all knew of Mother's Dream House, as we called it, and used to tease her about it. Well, last year she went, with our father, to view a shooting-box in Scotland—this very Oban Lodge you stayed in—and, the moment she saw it, she recognized her Dream House. That was strange enough, you'll admit. But when the owners of the Lodge saw her, they exclaimed: 'Why, this is our ghost!' and told her how they had seen her for years haunting the corridors."

"How very extraordinary! The ghost who opened my door at the Gillespies hadn't been alive for about two hundred years—quite an ordinary, Christmas-story ghost. But a live one—I mean one still in the flesh—I've never heard of before. At least, I've heard of people recognizing places they'd seen in dreams, of course, but not of their being recognized as haunting phantoms—or 'phantasms,' as you call them."

"I don't call them anything. I haven't thought much about them. It is Myers' term, not mine. To my mind the most curious part of the whole story is that Emily should have happened to be called in, out of all the artists in London, to paint the little lady with grey curls who had opened her door at Oban Lodge!"

Peggy reflected a moment. "It makes one think, doesn't it?" she said: "Where do we go in our dreams? Is it a fact, as spiritualists declare, that we leave our bodies and wander afield? I don't care much for the idea, do you?"

"No. But if it isn't so, how do you account for this story?"

"I don't account for it. Any more than I can account for the noises last night. If we rule out all supernatural manifestation there is no possible way of accounting for such phenomena, is there?"

"There may be a quite scientific explanation, that we shall know some day. We're learning all sorts of things about 'sound-waves' and 'light-waves' that our mothers knew nothing of. They may finally account for apparitions in the air—who knows?"

They left it at that, and the subject was not opened again. But Percy remarked casually at lunch, when Cookie was in the room:

"I wish those people in Heddon Road would keep their beastly dogs quiet at night. If they don't, I shall have to complain. Sickening to be disturbed by the brutes just when one is dropping off to sleep."

His grin when the door closed on Cookie was one of complete satisfaction.

"There, I hope that has squelched the dog spook nonsense," he said. "If our dear domestic treasures begin to get the wind up, we shall be left alone a-mourning; and don't you forget it, Peg. It is our business to see that their innocent minds are not disturbed by ghostly apprehensions."

That afternoon they went to a *Thé Dansant* at the "White Hart," meeting by appointment a young architect named Spencer, with whom Percy had fraternized at golf, and the four had a very jolly dance together. They dined at the hotel and went afterwards to the Picture Palace to see an excellent film of *Pickwick*, which afforded them a great laugh. What with the dancing and the laughing, and the almost sleepless night before, the girls were very tired when they got home. They sat round the fire, eating sandwiches and drinking hot drinks till long after midnight; too lazy to take the trouble of walking upstairs and undressing. Percy was chock-full of Dickens and could quote him by the yard. He could also impersonate the characters, and when once a Dickens lover starts talking about that inimitable author, he doesn't know how to stop. The room was cosy in the lamp-light, the fire cheery, and it was Joan's last night at "Hell Corner." Grandfather on the stairs had tolled the half-hour before they roused themselves and went to bed. Nothing disturbed them, and all were asleep almost as soon as their heads touched their pillows.

And next day Joan Millis went home.

CHAPTER XIV

FOR some time Peggy heard nothing to make her heart beat a shade faster or raise the question always in her mind as to the possibility, or impossibility, or spiritualistic manifestation. Were all the phenomena of lore and legend, and the séance, purely subjective, freaks of individual fancy or 'nerve storms'? She asked herself this frequently, and, as the vivid impressions of the last strange happenings gradually faded, was inclined to believe that Percy was right, and her own senses wrong. Had she not only imagined the noises she had heard but, with subtle thought-transference, managed to suggest them to Joan and the maids? The sounds Cookie had heard might have been nothing more supernatural than her own moving about the house, when she had gone into Joan's room; and the barking might have come, as Percy suggested, from a house a little way off. The power of suggestion, she knew, was great; even Percy did not entirely disbelieve in it; and it was quite possible she had put the idea into Nanny's mind. It would account, also, for other things. How far, for instance, had she herself been influenced by Susan Cleaver, who had suggested that her late master haunted the house? It is true she had felt from the first there was something uncanny, and the children had seen and heard things. But children are extraordinarily given to inventing fictions of their own, and her children were particularly gifted in that way. The "funny old man" in the garden might be only one more of Gib's imaginative conceptions. She tried hard to believe this, to shake off the continuous dread she felt of hearing or seeing something mysterious and unaccountable.

She had almost succeeded when all her fears were roused again, and her conviction that the house was haunted so solidly confirmed that she had no more questions or doubts on the subject.

It was about a fortnight after Joan Millis had left, and Peggy's mind was full of approaching Christmastide. She thought continually of Christmas presents and was working hard to finish things she was making for her friends and for her own and other people's children—dainty little garments, vanity bags, handkerchief sachets, jumpers, socks, frocks, and petticoats for dolls, etc. She had made a magnificent Jumbo for Billikin and was dressing an exquisite baby doll for Fliss, putting almost as much pleasure into the tiny robe as she had put into her own baby things. Gib had, alas! outgrown her manufactures and must have a wheelbarrow or a cricket bat. She and Percy had not quite decided on his present, or on K.'s.

Percy had gone to town, to a special dinner given to the staff of the paper for which he chiefly worked. But Peggy did not feel lonely: she was too busy. Absorbed in her work she sat up long after the maids had gone to bed, stitching away with a smile on her lips at pleasant thoughts and anticipations. Suddenly she shivered and looked up to find that the fire was nearly out and the clock on the mantelpiece pointed to past midnight.

As she went upstairs all her old apprehensions returned in full force. Grandfather, half-way up, gave her a fearful start by striking the quarter just as she reached him, and she shuddered away nervously, thinking how a goblin, or other strange creature from the unseen world, might easily lie hidden in his big lacquer case. But once in her room, with a glowing fire for company—this being a special occasion for such a luxury—Peggy felt no more qualms. Her mind was full of a hundred small matters. First the usual things that engage a woman's thoughts, when she is a housekeeper and mother; the next day's meals, the children's needs, the orders to be given to tradespeople, the work to be done. Then such questions as should K. wear her little white frock for the children's party to which she was invited next Friday, or the warmer pink knitted one? What colour would look best to line the nightdress case she was making for Joan? And what on earth was she to give Perks this year? She had given him socks last year, when he was low in socks. Now he seemed to have everything he wanted. It was a most knotty question and she pondered over it a good deal. She felt doubtful about the style she had chosen for her new evening frock and wondered whether it might not make her look short. The dressmaker said not, but dressmakers generally say what they think you will like to hear. This question worried her a good deal. Peggy could not afford many frocks so it was most important to get one that suited her.

Then her thoughts strayed to other matters. Was she really improving at golf, as Mr. Spicer said? Or was he only saying it to please her? She thought she had improved a little. The book by H. G. Wells she had just finished was disappointing. Clever and amusing of course, but not what one expected from so exceptional a writer. Would it be possible, as Percy had suggested, to go up to town for a matinée of Bernard Shaw's play before it was taken off? If only she and Percy could write a book together, with illustrations by him, what fun it would be! And they might make some money by it. She was full of ideas, and so was he; it was only a question of stringing them together.

As she began to attempt this her thoughts became a jumble and she was dropping away from them into sleep when a sound below jerked her wide awake again, and she held her breath to listen.

There could be no doubt whatever that some one—or *something*—

was moving about below. She thought at first it was in the hall; then in the room beneath the drawing-room that ran the length of her own room and the day nursery. Her heart began to beat fast. She knew that she ought to get up and go down. There might be burglars stealing the silver, and Percy would think her a dreadful coward if she let them off without so much as an alarm. But she felt paralysed; as if no power on earth could make her stir from her bed. It was easy to find excuses for not going down. If she did, and if there were house-breakers, they might murder her. Imagination, thereupon, sketched a tragic picture of herself lying dead, in a pool of blood, at the foot of the stairs, with her children shrieking round her and begging her to wake up. The conjuration was so vivid that tears came to her eyes and she found herself speculating as to how Percy would take her untimely demise. Would he be prostrated with grief? Would he marry again? She listened and shook with mingled self-pity and terror.

Then she pulled herself together and muttered aloud: "I am a fool. Of course it is not burglars. I know it is not burglars. I know it is——"

But there she paused, not daring to face her thought.

There was another sound below, as of furniture being shifted, and then—silence; broken only by the thud, thud of her heart in her ears. Her skin grew damp and she felt faint. She longed for a cock to crow, but there was no sound outside. Nor was there any further disturbance from within. As the minutes passed into an hour her heart ceased thumping and her fears subsided. She grew sleepy and, before the cock crowed, she slept.

. . . . .

She thought of her terror the moment she awoke. Indeed, the morning knock on her door gave her a new shock of fear and sent a tremor through her nerves. But, bathed and dressed, she could laugh at herself and throw off the dread obsession of the night.

There were happier things to think of. She could hear her darlings chattering over their breakfast in the nursery, and ran in for her morning kiss, to be greeted by Billikin with "Hallo, Peggy!" and his funny little grin of sheer delight at seeing her, which always warmed her heart. He always called her Peggy in his laughing moods; only in trouble he called for Mummie! Who could brood upon ghosts and hauntings with that happy little quartet in the nursery, and the prospect of welcoming a precious husband home in a few hours? She found some interesting letters, too, beside her plate and the newspaper had a full account of the dinner last night in its columns. Percy's name was there, side by side with several distinguished artists and men of letters. She felt a simple glow of pride in him—her clever Perks.

But all her pleasant thoughts were scattered when Cookie brought in her coffee and scrambled egg.

"Did you come down in the night, 'm?" she asked.

"No. Why?" Peggy exclaimed quickly.

"I thought some one must have been in the drawing-room. Things weren't in their usual places," replied Cookie. "Do you think anyone could have got in, 'm?"

Peggy sprang up and rushed into the drawing-room. It appeared quite normal, and as she had left it the night before. She said so.

"Oh yes, 'm. I put it all straight, of course. But the sofa was drawn up by the fireplace, the chairs were all anyhow and that there fire-screen stood in the middle of the room."

Peggy turned suddenly icy cold and shivered. Then she looked at her table of silver things, almost hoping to find them gone. But no—they were all there. Nothing had been taken from the room.

"I wish you had left it for me to see," she said. "Whereabouts was the screen?"

"Just here, 'm." Cook stood in about the middle of the room. "It looked so funny there that it struck me directly I opened the door. But I thought you might have shifted it out of its place in the night, if you came down to look for anything."

"I——" Peggy was just going to say, "I didn't," when she remembered Percy's warning. If she didn't move it, who did? It would never do to let Cookie think it had been moved by supernatural agency. She cleared her throat and said: "I may have moved it when I was dusting yesterday, but I don't remember doing so . . . . I did push the sofa about a bit, I think . . . . But my breakfast is getting cold. What about lunch? I am not quite sure Mr. Dacre will be home in time, but we must have something nice that can be kept hot, in case he turns up late."

For the sake of the children they generally had hot meat and vegetables in the middle of the day and a light dinner at night. Peggy went back to her breakfast, which she ate mechanically and without much appetite. All her old terrors had returned in full force. She had no longer any doubt whatever that some superhuman force was at work; and while she puzzled over it—for it seemed absurd to think of the immaterial using dynamic energy against the material, and a spiritual being to move furniture—she could not shake off the conviction that this inconceivable thing had, nevertheless, happened. And she resolved, then and there, to have this out with Percy; to tell him exactly what had occurred and say that he must either believe her word or denounce her as a liar. He would not do that, she knew, but she felt there would be a tussle between them and the thought of this spoilt her pleasure in his home-coming.

But something must be done. She could not go on living in a haunted house and liable to be terrified out of her life at any moment. Worse even than that was the fear that the maids might be frightened and give notice; worse still, that her darlings might be frightened. She had heard of children having epileptic fits after a violent fright. So far they had accepted the "funny old man" in the garden as a real person. But suppose they woke up in the night and found him standing by their beds? And if old Barker had the power to materialize at all, why should he not do so at any time, and in any place?

Yes, she must have it out with Percy and something must be done, or she would leave the house and take the children with her. But as to what *could* be done, she had not the remotest idea. Joan's suggestion of exorcism was the only solution of the problem that occurred to her, but she was well aware that Percy would scoff at the idea of asking a priest, with bell, book and candle, to come into his house and cure it of 'spooks.'

He turned up just as she was sitting down to lunch, very jolly and full of last night's proceedings; the people he had met, the speeches he had heard, the wine he had drunk. He assured her that he had gone to bed with his shoes on and laid his head where his feet ought to be, but the twinkle in his eyes would have betrayed him even if Peggy had not been used to these fictions, or known him to be the most abstemious of men. She pretended to be shocked, of course, to please him, and listened to all his jocund talk till he was tired of talking; only too glad to put off the evil hour in which she must tell him her fears and her resolve. By that time it was the children's hour and he romped with them till their bed-time. It was not until after dinner that Peggy found the dreaded moment in which to tackle him. But it came at last, and her voice shook a little as she said, after a pause in their conversation:

"You seem to have had a very jolly evening last night, and I loved hearing all about it. But *I* didn't have a jolly evening at all, and now you've got to hear about it."

"Sorry, darling. What a shame! Fire away!" he said. And Peggy started firing.

CHAPTER XV

PEGGY launched out into a full description of her night terrors and Percy listened with that quizzical smile on his lips she knew so well and hated to see. It meant that he discounted everything she said, not as falsehood or fiction, for he knew she earnestly believed all she told him, but as a pure figment of her over-vivid imagination. He made no comment, however, until she went on to tell him of Cook's discovery that morning, when he said, with a decidedly surprised look in his eyes:

"Do you mean to say that she actually asked you if you had moved the furniture before you mentioned having been disturbed in the night? Come now, Pegtop, you said something to her first about it. Own up."

"I did *not*, Percy. After your warning the other day, do you think I should be so foolish as to frighten either of the maids? Surely you give me credit for more sense than that. On the contrary, when she assured me the furniture had been moved I told her I had probably done it myself, when I was dusting in the morning."

"Perhaps you did."

"And perhaps I did *not*. Why should I move that heavy Chesterfield half across the room, and set the fire-screen in the middle of it? And leave it there all day!"

"It seems to me just as likely as that a spook could move it. How could an immaterial thing move a material one?"

"Why not? Doesn't steam move trains and electric current drive engines? Should you call them material things?"

Percy laughed. "You have me there, dazzling Star of Light. But, at least, you will admit that you are capable of absent-mindedness at times, and might have manipulated things in the room without remembering afterwards, if suddenly called away for something."

"I admit that I am capable of anything silly, as you seem to think."

"There you are wrong, my Life. It isn't silly to be absent-minded. On the other hand, it may be a sign of genius. I believe your silliness to be wiser than most people's wisdom, I assure you. But, to return. What did Cookie say when you told her you might have shifted the Chesterfield? Did she believe you?"

"I don't know. She didn't say. I expect so. Simple people will believe the most absurd statement rather than own a thing is unaccountable."

The cut at Percy was too obvious to be missed by him and he chuckled again.

"Be thankful you've got a simple husband, Peg o' my Heart, and not one of those clever pigs who would dare to argue with you. Have you, by any chance, counted the silver?"

"Of course I have. Didn't I tell you I'd looked all round. There's nothing missing."

He looked thoughtful. "Well, it's a queer business, I admit. The only solution to the mystery I can think of is that some one is trying to frighten us. Some one who wants the house, perhaps. and thinks he'll get us out of it by such scares. People will go to almost any lengths to get a house in these days. You may depend upon it somebody has heard that you are nervous and have heard strange noises. They, or he—whoever it was—got into the house last night, and that other night when you and Joan were frightened. I'll put the matter into the hands of the police and get them to watch. We shall soon catch the ghost," he concluded cheerfully.

Peggy was struck dumb. What could one say to such a doubting Thomas as this? It seemed to her far more credulous to believe that some man—he must be a man of their own class, with means to take such a house as this—would risk being caught as a burglar and brought before a magistrate in his own town, rather than that a conscience-stricken spirit, cut off suddenly from the world before he had accomplished an act of justice, should haunt the house. As she said to Joan, such a form of scepticism, dependent on believing absurdities, was beyond her ken. But Percy was built that way. There was nothing too ridiculous for him to believe rather than give credence to anything supernatural. Religion had been spoilt for him by the miracles in the Bible. He trusted the evidence of his own senses, and the reasoning of his own mind, but nothing else in the world.

"Of course you tried all the doors and window fastenings?" he said now.

Peggy was caught. She hadn't thought of this and had to say so. Thereupon he strode from the room to examine all the drawing-room windows, and exclaimed triumphantly:

"I thought as much!" A side window was unfastened. They were sash windows, with patent, burglar-proof catches, put there by the late owner.

"That is the window Cookie always opens when she does the room in the morning," said Peggy. "No doubt she left it unfastened then."

"I don't think so! But we won't ask her; it might arouse her suspicions and scare her."

"Not likely. If we could prove some one had got in, it might allay any fear she already has, rather than cause it."

She rang the bell and Cookie came in.

"Did you forget to fasten the side window in the drawing-room, when you shut it this morning?" asked Peggy.

"I don't think so, 'm. I always do fasten it when I shut it. Yes, I'm sure I did."

"Are you sure you opened it?" queried Percy.

"Oh yes, sir, I——" she stopped abruptly. "Which window did you find unfastened?" she asked.

They went back to the drawing-room and showed her. Cookie thought a few moments.

"I don't believe I opened this one," she said, then: "I'm almost sure I didn't. It was the other side one I opened this morning, because the rain was that side. Yes, 'm, I remember now. This is the window I opened and shut. It's fastened now, see——"

"Then the other was unfastened all night, as I thought," remarked Percy, quietly, but with a finality most irritating to his wife.

"Was it sir? I'm very sorry if I forgot it. It was careless of me. Anybody might have got in."

Then, as she was going out of the door, the girl turned and exclaimed:

"Why, I wonder if anyone did. That would account for things being all anyhow, 'm, wouldn't it? And if they did——"

"It's all right, Cookie, nothing has been taken," Peggy said. "I looked all round this morning, you know. Perhaps some one got in and had an alarm while he was hunting about. We must be more careful in future."

When Cook had gone out, Percy observed:

"It is quite obvious that the intruder wasn't a burglar. My theory holds good."

Peggy stared at him a moment.

"You really believe that, Perks?"

"Why not, my most valued Treasure?"

"Believe that some well-to-do man, a neighbour, perhaps, broke into our house last night for the sole purpose of frightening us out of it?"

"Frightening *you*, my Angel, not *us*. No doubt he knew I was away."

Peggy gave a little snort of contempt.

"You are extraordinarily credulous, Perks," she said.

"Credulous! Me!" he looked surprised.

"Yes, you. If you can believe that, you can believe anything," she retorted.

"You're wrong, my Candid Critic. I can't believe in ghosts!" he replied. "And my reason tells me that heavy furniture doesn't jazz about a room by itself."

"I'd just as soon believe in jazzing furniture as that any respectable man would risk his reputation by climbing in at the window of another man's house and shoving his things about to scare a woman in bed. *It isn't done*, Percy!"

"People would do anything for a house nowadays. He would think it a lark—an adventure."

Peggy shrugged her shoulders. It was impossible to argue with Percy. Then a thought struck her.

"It was a wet night last night. Rather strange that Cookie found no marks on the carpet this morning, if a man got in at the window," she shrugged.

"Are you sure she didn't?"

"She would have told me."

Percy examined the carpet near the window carefully and fancied he saw a crumb of garden mould. Then he went out into the garden with a pocket torch and scrutinized the flower-bed under it.

"I believe I can see a footprint," he said, with a slight shiver, when he came in, for it was very wet and cold.

"You'd believe anything you wished to believe, Perks, like all biased people," she remarked. He laughed.

"True enough, oh Fount of Wisdom. Who doesn't?" he said. "Anyhow, we'll see in the morning. If I show you a solid human footprint, will you still accuse your Percival of credulity and put faith in your spook?"

"If you find a footprint directly under the window, I will certainly recant," she replied, "but if you don't—what then? Will you admit that your theory of a gentleman-housebreaker is squashed?"

"Not at all," he answered promptly. "because the rain will probably have washed out the footprint. What?"

"You are simply a fanatic!" she exclaimed, laughing. "The early Christian martyrs weren't in it with you for blind faith and obstinacy. Cling to your old theory, then, and I'll cling to mine, which is, at least, based on the evidence of my own senses. Yours has no basis whatever, but is merely an invention of your fertile mind."

They wrangled no more on the subject. Peggy, who knew Percy perhaps as well as a woman can ever know a man, came to the conclusion that he did not really put much faith in his theory of a gentleman-housebreaker, but that he thought she, being a simple woman, might be induced to believe in it. It was what he would have called "window-dressing," designed to take her in. She wasn't being taken in, however. Simple she might be, in many little feminine ways, which to him only added to her attractions, but easily duped she was not. Extremely wide awake was Margaret Dacre and he who would catch her napping must sit up all night! She was fully awake to the absurdity of Percy's suggestion, as he soon realized.

Nevertheless, having made it, he was obliged to carry on; and next morning they both went out into the garden to examine the flower-border round the drawing-room window. There was no sign of a footprint. The forget-me-nots and pink double daisies that were planted there, to support the tulips in spring, showed no pressure anywhere on their dull and wintry leaves. Even Percy had to admit that. He went through the farce of pushing the window up and setting a knee on the sill, to show it could be done without treading on the flower-bed, but Peggy only laughed and said:

"Bunkered, old dear! You know as well as I do that you haven't a leg to stand on."

"Of all the unbelieving sceptics I ever knew, you, my Ray of Moonlight, are the worst," he declared. "Haven't I shown you quite clearly how the house could be entered by that unlatched window? And here—yes,—I thought so—here is a cigarette-end to prove my words."

He stooped, as he spoke, to pick up the object mentioned and, for the moment, Peggy was cornered. Then she took it from him and laughed.

"A perfectly dry one that has been out in the rain all night," she said. "Another miracle, Perks! Where is the cigarette you were smoking when we came out?"

CHAPTER XVI

THE following weeks were very busy ones for them both. Percy had some fresh orders and was drawing steadfastly through all the hours of daylight. Peggy had her home-made gifts to finish and others to choose at Leatheringham. On one of two days she drove herself in the car over to the county town and did some of her shopping there. She was coming out of a shop in Leatheringham a few days before Christmas when she met Susan Cleaver and stopped to speak with her, impelled by an impulse of sympathy, for the woman looked very shabby and wretched; much more so than she had done the last time Peggy had seen her.

"How are you?" she enquired. "You don't look very well to-day."

"I am all right, thank you, ma'am, I've had a bad cold, but it's going off. How are the children, and Mr. Dacre, ma'am? None the worse for this cold and damp weather, I trust."

"No; they are splendid, thanks, and I hope they'll keep so over Christmas now. Of course, they're wildly excited at the thought of Christmas. It's the children's time, isn't it? I'm just getting some things for their tree. I bought most of them a week ago, but I wanted a few more."

The woman smiled wistfully. "How they will love it, the little dears! I haven't seen a Christmas-tree for thirty years, or more. May I contribute something to it, Mrs. Dacre? It would be such a pleasure."

"Of course you may. And come to see it, too. Shall you be here for Christmas, or do you go to stay with friends?"

Susan smiled again—the same sad wistful smile that went to Peggy's heart.

"I don't seem to have any friends left," she said. "I suppose I lost them all when I was staying at The Beeches. You see, Mr. Barker never liked me to go anywhere, or ask anyone in; so I never did."

("The old curmudgeon!" Peggy thought.)

Aloud she said:

"Then you're going to spend Christmas in your rooms? But not alone, I hope?"

"Yes, ma'am. As it happens, I shall be quite alone. For Mrs. Stubbs, my landlady, is going to spend the day with her married daughter. But she has promised to provide me with a nice dinner, so I shall be all right in that way. I'm used to a quiet Christmas, you know."

"Why not come and spend it with us?" exclaimed Peggy, impulsively. "I am sure Cookie and Nanny will be delighted to have another visitor. Cookie is having her sister to stay with her, so you would make a nice little quartet in the kitchen. What do you say?"

For a moment Peggy was afraid the dignified and severe-looking woman was going to dissolve into tears. They sprang to her eyes, and a flush to her cheeks as Susan replied:

"You are too kind, Mrs. Dacre. I don't know how to thank you." Her voice cracked a bit, and she went on shakily. "But shan't I be in the way and spoil your merry party? I'm such a wet blanket these days?"

"Nothing of the kind. I want you to come. I don't like to think of anyone being lonely at Christmas, if I can help it. Besides, I know you'll help a bit, and there will be lots to do. As for being a wet blanket, we'll dry you with a warm welcome."

Susan Cleaver turned aside to blow her nose. Then she said again:

"You are too good to me, ma'am. Of course there is nothing I should like so much as to spend Christmas at the old house I've lived in for so many years, and with such a happy family. And you know I shall be only too glad to help in any way. If the girls like to go out, I could stay in and wash up."

"That's an idea!" exclaimed Peggy. "And really, I was thinking I must get some one in to help. But I made sure you would be away. I am glad you can come. Good-bye now till Christmas morning."

She went on her way, pleased to have been able to do a kindness for a forlorn fellow-creature. Her statement that she had been thinking of getting outside help was not entirely fiction, but she had not decided to do so, her mind being full of so many things. Now the matter seemed to have been decided for her, she felt extremely satisfied with herself. Both her maids liked Susan Cleaver. When she told them of the invitation Cookie expressed approval.

"Poor soul, she will enjoy it," was her comment; to which she added naïvely, "and help with the washing-up."

Upon which Peggy realized, for the first time, that this had been the fly in the kitchen ointment!

On Christmas Eve they had 'waits' of various kinds.[10] All the week there had been groups of small boys and girls ringing the door-bell violently and long, after bawling a few verses of *Good King Wenceslas*, or *While Shepherds Watched*, on the door-step, out of time and tune, very perfunctorily and with considerable haste to get on to the next house. They expected largesse for these distressing and inharmonious efforts, and Peggy, brought up in all the old Christmastide traditions, persisted in responding with pennies, against the wishes of Percy, who cursed them as a nuisance—which they were. But on Christmas Eve these gave place to bands and choirs and bell-ringers, who handed in books to be

---

10 Waits: groups of singers or musicians who sing or play carols for money.

signed and expected nothing less than silver. They gave more or less melodious renderings of the old carols, and Peggy enjoyed their performances, which appealed, perhaps, to her emotions more than to her musical taste.

The bell-ringers asked to be allowed to come into the hall, a custom, Peggy was given to understand, hallowed for many years in the larger houses of the town. Their finely toned instruments, they declared, were susceptible to cold and damp; so that, unless admitted into the house, they could not give their programme. Mr. Barker, it appeared, had always invited them in; they were almost the only people who ever were invited in, one of the bell-ringers remarked, and, as Peggy whispered to her husband:

"If that old curmudgeon let them in, we can't do less."

She was glad they had done so when they saw the delight of the children, who were permitted to sit up an hour over their usual bed-time because it was Christmas Eve. And the bell-ringers afforded her and Percy great amusement. They were a curiously assorted little party, of different sizes and ages, and the tense earnestness of their faces, as they watched each other and kept their places in the tune, was quite fascinating. Percy made several little sketches of them in his notebook which afterwards appeared in a magazine article, but they did not see him doing it. Indeed, they seemed scarcely aware of any other living creature while they played. No virtuoso, enchanting the public with his genius, could have looked more rapt and inspired than these good fellows playing *O come, all ye Faithful*, or *The Mistletoe Bough* on their silvery toned but terribly ringing instruments. Percy and Peggy, who had both sensitive nerves, found their resonance too penetrating and retired to the back of the drawing-room to listen; but the maids and children were enthralled and closed round the performers with wondering eyes and delighted ears. They had never seen or heard anything like this before.

Percy offered the men drinks, but they declined. It was too early in the evening and they had too many calls to make, said their spokesman.

"If we began taking drinks now we shouldn't see straight before we'd done," he said, and this was regarded as a witticism by the rest. They went forth again highly satisfied with their reception and the sum recorded in their subscription book.

"I suppose they ring the church bells all the year for nothing and this is their only reward," observed Percy. "Curious form of pleasure that. But they seem to enjoy it vastly."

They were all round the fire now, and the door closed, for the room had got rather chilly. Billikin had jumped on his mother's knee and was playing with her amber beads. Fliss, on Daddy's knee, leaned a little fluffy head against his shoulder and the two bigger children squatted on the rug between them.

"I wonder why one old man didn't have any bells," remarked Gib.

"What's that, my son?" asked Percy. Gib repeated his observation.

"Why, they all had bells, Gib. Didn't you see them?"

"Not one of them didn't," said Gilbert, "the one who stood in the doorway."

Peggy felt an icy shiver run up her spine. The hall had a glass partition and door between it and the front door, forming a small vestibule. The glass door had been open, the outer one, of course, closed.

"Silly boy!" said Percy, with a quick glance at his wife. "Why do you make such things up? You know there wasn't anyone in the doorway."

"There was, Daddy," Gib assured him earnestly. "You saw him, too, didn't you K.?"

"Yes, I did," asseverated K.; "and I knew him again too dreckly. It was the same old man we've seen in the garden. But he hadn't any bells really, Daddy. I wonder why he hadn't?"

For the first time Peggy noted a look of strange discomfort pass, like a shadow, over her husband's usually imperturbable face.

"What was the old man like? Was he like me at all?" he asked.

"Oh, no, Daddy, not a bit"—both the children laughed at the bare idea. "He's quite old, with a beard and a funny face."

"He has starting eyes," said K.

"And smiles, like this, all the time," added Gib, with a silly grin.

Peggy felt colder and colder.

"He's such a funny old man," murmured Fliss, sleepily.

At this moment Nanny came in to fetch the two babies.

"Did you see anyone come into the hall to-night beside the bell-ringers, Nanny?" asked Percy.

"No, sir, there wasn't anyone else," she replied. Peggy drew a short breath of relief.

"Come, Billikin—come to Nanny, darling. Come, Fliss," said the nurse, taking the baby boy in her arms.

"Stay 'ere," said Fliss.

"I thought perhaps they might have brought some one with them, to carry their bags," Percy went on. "You didn't see anyone?"

"No, sir. I'm sure nobody else came in. Did you think there was?"

"No, but Gib and K. thought they did."

A glint of alarm came into the girl's eyes. "They are always fancying things—or making them up," she said.

"We don't!" exclaimed Gib, indignantly. "We saw the old man quite plainly, both of us. Didn't we K.?"

"Yes, we did."

There was a moment's silence. Then Percy laughed.

"Of course I know what you saw, children. It was the reflection in the glass partition of the fat old bell-ringer with the beard. Now I come to think of it, I saw it too. Now my little white bunnie must leave her Dad and go to bye-byes. We mustn't keep poor Nanny waiting any longer. If you don't go now, and do as you're told, Father Christmas won't come and fill your stocking to-night, you know. He has no truck with naughty children. Just see how fast you can get upstairs—shoo!"

Fliss was chased from the room, shrieking with laughter. There was a shuffling of feet and sound of voices outside, after which a very raucous band started *Christians, Awake!* in a manner to have the desired effect. Gib and K. rushed to the window and there stood peeping behind the curtain delightedly, while their parents listened to the cacophony without hearing it. Both their minds were busily working over "the old man with a beard"; for Percy believed no more in his theory of a reflection than Peggy did. He was frankly puzzled. But he had no intention of saying so.

The front door-bell rang; the usual little dirty account book was handed in. Percy handed out a piece of silver with a grimace.

"You might give them a hint that the babies are in bed, and so we must deprive ourselves of the pleasure of a further selection," he said to Cookie, and as the girl went out, he added *sotto voce*:

"I'm just wondering, Peg, whether music was not, after all, an invention of the Devil. I've had enough this evening to last me till next year."

"Oh, Daddy!" the two children exclaimed together, and Gib, after a moment's reflection, observed that music couldn't be the Devil's invention, or they wouldn't have it in church.

Soon after that the two elder children went to bed, and Percy fetched in the Christmas tree from its hiding-place in the garage.

CHAPTER XVII

THERE may be supercilious persons inclined to laugh at the childish couple, who enjoyed so much dressing a Christmas-tree for their offspring; but their laugh might well be the scoff of envy, and certainly our Percy and Peggy would be the last to mind their scorn. To be able to find joy in small things is a gift direct from the gods, and only vouchsafed to their special favourites.

To hear this couple discussing how and where to hang all the cheap toys Peggy had bought during the last fortnight, you might have thought it a quite serious matter whether the flag, above Father Christmas at the top, should stand over the Star of Bethlehem or wave beneath it; whether it would do to hang the doll's cradle and a tin motor-car on one branch, or replace the latter by a silver bell; whether there were more candles on one side or the other, and many more knotty questions. When the wonderful thing was finished, the happy pair stood gazing on it with supreme satisfaction. They even had to call in the maids to admire their handiwork. And whether you scoff at it or not, you've got to admit that a Christmas-tree *is* a pretty thing, a picturesque thing, an object full of suggestion and old associations. Cold indeed must be the heart that does not feel a melting warmth at the sight of a Christmas-tree.

After dinner they started on the stockings. Peggy fetched down the four long white ones, which had been unearthed for her out of stores in the family, and a dress box full of toys and sweets. The fond parents spent another merry hour over this job, squabbling gaily over the distribution of the various articles, which seemed to require much earnest consideration. "This must go in Billy's";

"No, I want that for Fliss," was a continual bicker. They were all cheap things, a few shillings would have covered the cost of the lot. But Peg and Perks had no delusions about their children's taste. They knew well enough that a twopenny tin motor would give as much pleasure as a 'Meccano' train, though the pleasure might not last as long; and that the joy of giving their youngsters expensive presents was chiefly confined to themselves. *They* enjoyed playing with the 'Meccano' train, and other splendid toys immensely; whereas the children could be quite as happy with a few marbles, old brick puzzles and a half-empty box of dominoes.

A very beautifully dressed doll and cradle for K., a tiny tricycle for Gib, a wheelbarrow for Fliss—who loved pushing things about—and the Jumbo Peggy had made for Billikin, were ranged to meet the ravished eyes of the children when they came down for their hour in the morning-room, while Nanny tidied the night nursery; together with a stack of parcels that had come by post from kind friends and relatives.

While they were engaged on this serious and important work, Peggy and her husband were able to shake off the uncomfortable thoughts that had assailed them since Gib had spoken of the "funny old man" in the hall. But when the four long, white, distorted legs had been laid sprawling on the sofa (rather dreadful objects, it must be confessed) and the pair sat down by the fire, to smoke and drink hot lemonade, their minds again became a prey to perplexing doubts and queries.

"Perks, what do you really think about the old man the children saw?" asked Peggy, after a pause.

"Reflection in the glass screen," he replied, promptly. "I remember seeing it."

"The truth, Percy. Of course I know it was necessary to say

that to Nanny and the children; but it isn't to me. Confess now, honestly, you were taken aback."

"I was till I thought it out."

"You can convince yourself of anything you wish to believe, I know. But is it reasonable to suppose that Gib would not know a real man from a reflection in the glass? Do you really think your eldest child is an idiot?"

"He is very imaginative."

"What about K.?"

"She would back up anything Gib said."

"There you are wrong. She loves to contradict him flatly."

A short pause ensued. They were both thinking hard. Then Percy said:

"Well now, Moon of my Delight, let's hear what *you* think it was, if it wasn't a reflection or a shadow."

"You know what I think, Percy."

She spoke in a low voice.

"A spook?"

"Yes, if you like to call it so. A silly American word, I think, with no appreciable derivation. Isn't ghost a good enough old Anglo-Saxon word for you?"

He didn't answer; only laughed.

"You may call it what you like," Peggy went on, "but the fact remains that those children see something we can't see, or *you* can't. I've seen it once."

"When?"

"The day of my Bridge Drive. I saw it outside in the garden."

Percy smiled, the superior smile that always irritated Peggy. "Life of my Soul, you are as full of superstition as an egg is full of meat," he said, "I really don't know what to do with you."

"Why should you call it 'superstition'?" she demanded vehemently: "You don't know everything, any more than I do. And the ether, or whatever it is, of which our spiritual bodies consist, may be governed by perfectly natural laws that we have yet to understand. Have you ever reflected that the scoffing sceptic's attitude is that of the fool who said in his heart 'there is no God'?"

"Do you mean me by 'the scoffing sceptic'?" enquired her husband, pleasantly. "I rather like that alliterative title."

"Don't be flippant, Perks. I am talking seriously. If you had lived a few hundred years ago nothing on earth would have made you believe that the world was round."

"Perhaps it isn't. Some one will be getting up some day to prove that it is flat, or square, or oblong. Who knows? And you would be one of the first to believe him!"

"I hope so!" Peggy retorted. "I hope my mind will never be closed to further realms of knowledge and unknown possibilities. And you cannot deny that if you'd lived even fifty years ago you wouldn't have believed that people could ever talk from one continent to another, or that you could hear music in Manchester that was played in London."

"You are quite right; I shouldn't," responded Percy, imperturbably.

"You would have thought it absurd, incredible, ridiculous, superstitious nonsense."

"I should," said Percy. "So would you."

Peggy had to smile. She was frank enough with herself to make an inward confession, at least, that she would have found the wireless miracle hard to swallow if it had not been demonstrated to her through her own ears.

"I'm sure I should not have said, even then, that anything could not be, in this changing world of wonders," she said aloud: "and

I should have tried to keep an open mind, if even I had doubts."

"We all think our own minds are open," said Percy, "and pride ourselves on the fact. But what does it amount to, after all? What *is* an open mind? Isn't it merely a credulous, unstable mind? I prefer to keep a chain on mine and open it an inch at a time, to peep through."

"Very well, then. Open it an inch now and admit that if our ears can be assisted to hear what is being said, or sung, a hundred miles away, there may be some means of hearing, or seeing, things in our immediate neighbourhood that are not seen or heard by everybody. You must be aware that there is a very large body of opinion all over the world, not entirely confined to the most ignorant and foolish people, who believe in communication with spiritual beings, and think we have not yet reached the limit of our knowledge on the subject."

He listened to this tirade attentively, and the smile faded from his lips.

"Your arguments are cogent, if not unanswerable, my Love Bird," he said at last. "I admit my inability to controvert them. But I was born a prosaic, marrer-of-fact oaf, with a shut-up mind and a rooted dislike to changing my opinions. I'll open half an inch, as the oyster does, to take in your pearls of wisdom and agree that there may be something in your philosophy. But I'll be hanged if I can believe that my children have seen a ghost. Why should it appear to them and not to me—who need conversion? If it has something to say and wants to get at us, for some reason or other, why doesn't it come out into the open and tackle me, instead of those little kids, who can't do anything—so far as I can see? There's no sense in appearing to Gib and K."

"Our minds—our senses—may not be tuned to see or hear

certain things, and the children's may. We couldn't hear music in London without the right medium, tuned to our hearing.

"Granted. I can only say, until I do actually see or hear something myself, I can't believe in spiritual manifestations."

"Doubting Thomas!" exclaimed Peggy.

"I've always thought there was a good deal to be said for Thomas," he observed. "He was a man rather like myself."

"And you think there is a good deal to be said for you!" she scoffed.

"A reasonable amount. Modesty forbids me stating such qualifications as I possess. You, my Own Guiding Star, may be left to fill them in."

She went over to him and sat down on his knee.

"There are times," she said, "when I positively detest you, and this is one of them."

To show this positive detestation she ruffled his hair and kissed his forehead.

"I accept your condemnation with resignation," he murmured.

"You are such a ridiculous old stick-in-the-mud," she declared.

"I am that."

"You won't believe anything that isn't stuck at the end of your nose," she urged.

"That's the worst of these long noses."

"You think your wife is a perfect fool."

"No, madam—not though she spends the best part of her time trying to convince me that she is."

"Don't you wish she had no imagination and no nerves; that she was matter-of-fact and stolid and bovine?"

"It would be a refreshing change."

"Ruffian!"

"But I should soon long for my own wee Will-o'-the-wisp back again. It is so diverting never to know what she will be up to next, or what new bee she will get in her bonnet."

"Then if you think——"

"I don't—it was only a figure of speech."

"*Good King Wenceslas looked out*——"

The sudden bawl of a mixed choir outside the window made them both jump and Peggy looked round in alarm to see whether the children had, by any chance, left a chink between the window curtains whereby those who came to entertain might be entertained. She sprang off her perch and took the chair opposite.

"May they all catch influenza, pneumonia, and appendicitis!" said Percy, charitably. "If only old Barker would haunt *them* he would be some use. I wonder they're not afraid to come here."

"He used to like them," Peggy said, laughing. "So Susan Cleaver says."

"He would—just what the old blighter *would* like. Damn that bell! I suppose the maids have gone to bed."

To the smiling, red-nosed group outside he expressed thanks for their delightful singing, but, as the children were asleep—and so forth. They withdrew, with a coin in the pouch, and a howl from above announced the effect of choral music on infant dreams.

Peggy and Percy cursed mildly together and waited for the sounds overhead to cease. How were those white, bulging legs to be disposed on cots where wakeful children were lying? The father and mother had to sit up nearly an hour longer. But old Barker was not discussed. Peggy was satisfied that, in spite of Percy's jeering, he had been impressed by Gib's assertion and was chewing it over in his mind.

CHAPTER XVIII

CHRISTMAS Day dawned serenely; one of the summer-like December Days that we have had for several years lately. The good, old-fashioned, snowy and frosty Christmastides we used to have, with skating and tobogganing, went out of the weather's fashion for a time and we had to be thankful when the sky was not grey with rain clouds. It was fine when the little family at The Beeches arose to open their stockings and parcels quite early, and the sun came out after breakfast.

The Dacre children, like all other children in the land, were wildly excited over the long, distorted legs that hung from the bottom rail of their cots and beds. In a very short time their rooms were in a froth of paper and bits of string, while a series of painful noises from tin trumpets, and 'musical' toys tortured the ears of the sensitive parents. It was worse when they came downstairs to open their parcels, for one kind and thoughtful friend had sent Billikin a large drum, which he beat without intermission, for half an hour on end, and at intervals all the morning; and another had sent Fliss a small chair which she dragged up and down the tessellated floor of the hall more or less all day!

Gib's tricycle, too, was hardly a silent witness, for it was unfortunately provided with a bell, and when he was not peddling about the halls and passages, he was ringing the bell. "Only trying it, Mummie," he said, in response to Peggy's protest; but it was necessary to try it often and long, according to Gib, and you can't spoil a child's pleasure on Christmas Day!

So long as their children were happy these doting parents were satisfied. What did anything else matter? K. was the only quiet one of the children. She gravitated between her doll, which she dressed and undressed about a dozen times, and a painting-book that, with a box of coloured crayons, had been brought her by Susan Cleaver. She could draw quite cleverly, for her age, and Peggy believed that she had inherited her father's gift. The painting-book was a nice one and engrossed her so much that her mother determined she should have a drawing-block and paint-box next Christmas.

Susan Cleaver appeared, with an unusually cheerful aspect, quite early in the morning and started to help the servants as soon as she arrived. She was one of those capable people who always seem to know exactly what is wanted, and what to do at any given moment, without being told. The dinner was arranged for 1.30 so that the children could dine with their parents, and a very merry dinner-party it was. Gib made a point of trying everything on the table, and a remark of his at the close of the feast is likely to be handed down as a family legend.

"What would you like now, darling?" asked his mother, after a banana, several prunes, and a pear had been despatched. And before Percy could utter the parental protest that rose to his lips, Gib replied:

"Let me see. What haven't I had?"

The parental protest ended in a shout of laughter, during which Gib reached out for a fig.

After dinner they went to the morning-room and played with their toys; each child in a corner to itself, the father and mother on their knees in the middle of the room trying to engage their interest in mechanical toys, especially the railway, which has a great fascination for parents. They had, however, more success with the shop, where Gib sold packets of tea and rice, K. put them in tiny paper bags, and Fliss trotted between her father, mother, and the shop as errand boy. This lasted till the dusk fell, when Mummie left the children with Daddy while she slipped into the drawing-room to light the candles on the Christmas-tree. The door had been kept locked, so that the tree could not be seen until the appointed time.

What a lovely sight it was, Peggy thought, standing in the middle of the green-decked room, with only the blazing firelight to help the twinkling coloured candles. The Star of Bethlehem glittered near Father Christmas and "Happy Christmas" could just be read on the flag above. It was not the children's first tree. Even Billikin, in his short life, had seen one last year from Nanny's arms. But this was bigger than usual, and isn't a Christmas-tree always fresh? The four children stood before it in rapt silence for some moments, gazing at it almost with awe, till Gib broke the spell by saying: "I should like the aeroplane," and K. followed suit by demanding Father Christmas himself from the top. Peggy was about to detach these delectables from the tree when Percy interposed firmly. "The tree is not to be touched," he said, solemnly, "until the proper rites have been performed. Nobody can have anything till after that, or Father Christmas would be deeply outraged. I, myself, am simply longing for that boat I see there, but I can't have it till we've gone through the usual ceremonies. Now, kids, join hands and dance round the tree with us. Come, Cookie, Nanny, Miss Cleaver, and sing out, all of you."

Then he began to jig round singing lustily:

"Here we go round the Christmas-tree,
The Christmas-tree, the Christmas-tree,
Here we go round the Christmas-tree
On a warm and muggy evening.

This is the way we dance and sing,
We dance and sing, we dance and sing,
This is the was we dance and sing
On a warm and muggy evening."

They all piped in: K. and Gib in a sweet treble, Fliss in a monotone, the elders more or less in tune, until the latter were out of breath. Then the dismantling of the tree began.

There were more presents for everybody, including the maids and Susan Cleaver. There were also presents for the Judkins children, and a slight altercation arose between Gib and K. as to who should present them, and what they should be; for of course there was something they wanted themselves among the toys set apart for the little Judkins.

"Bobby can have my cart—I've got another—and I'll have the windmill," said Gib.

"Dorothy can have my cradle and I'll have the fork and spoon," said K.

"You must take them the things we have—I mean Father Christmas has—ordained for them, or he will be deeply offended," declared Daddy. "But you may take them anything else you like as well."

This idea caught on, and the two elder children began to seek out things they did not care for themselves to go with the Judkins' toys from the tree. Unfortunately this led to some squabbling; for Gib wanted to choose things from K.'s collection to send, and K. wanted to send some from his.

"You've got ever so many dolls, K., so you'd better give one to Dorothy," urged Gib.

"You ought to give Bobby your engine, Gib, as you've got a whole train," K. declared. "Oughtn't he, Mummie?"

All this took place in the candlelight round the tree, while Peggy and Percy were hunting for anything that might still be hidden among the branches. A few sugar mice and chocolate babies were still concealed in shadowy parts.

Suddenly a low cry made them look up from their task to where Susan Cleaver was standing, with Cookie, by the piano. Susan had gripped Cookie's arm and was staring with wide-open eyes full of terror at the door opposite. Instinctively they all turned to see what she was gazing at.

There was nothing visible.

"What's the matter?" Percy asked, sharply. "Are you feeling ill, Miss Cleaver?"

"Ye-es. I had a spasm, sir," she replied, hoarsely, with an effort. Her face was white as chalk and her chin shook as if her teeth were chattering.

Peggy turned cold all over, from the roots of her hair to her feet. Her own teeth began to chatter. Fortunately the children were too much absorbed in their squabbling over the toys to notice anything.

Percy strode to the lamp and felt for his matches. What foolery was this? he said to himself, and what did the silly woman mean, frightening the other silly women? It was all due to this half-lighted room, full of shadows. But it was not only the 'silly women' who had been unnerved by that strangled shriek and horrified stare. Percy himself felt his hand shake as he lifted the glass chimney from the lamp and he was longer than usual fumbling over it before he could get it lighted.

"Miss Cleaver thought she saw something strange, she——" Cookie began, but Peggy interrupted any further speech by exclaiming:

"I expect dancing round the tree has upset her, in this bad light. It made me feel quite sick and giddy. I'll get her a little brandy."

Percy pushed forward an arm-chair and told Susan Cleaver to sit down. Then he turned to the maids.

"We must put out the candles now, or they'll be setting fire to the tree. I can smell burning leaves already. You know what to do—wet your fingers and pinch quickly. It won't hurt you. Like this."

While they were extinguishing the candles Susan slipped out of the room to the kitchen and sat down by the table, with clenched hands. There Cookie found her a few minutes later.

"What was it you saw, Miss Cleaver?" she asked, curiously, "I didn't see nothing, but I'm sure there's something funny about this house. The children have seen an old man about that nobody else sees. They saw him last night in the hall, when the bell-ringers were here. Mr. Dacre said it was a reflection in the glass; but I asked Gib about it again this morning and he was quite positive it wasn't in the glass."

Susan gave a little choke and gasp, clenching and unclenching her hands.

"It's right enough—it's right enough," she cried, rocking herself backwards and forwards in her chair. "He's come back! I knew he would. And now I've seen him, as clear as I see you."

Peggy, carrying a small glass of brandy and water, came into the kitchen at that moment and caught Susan's last words. They filled her with fear and consternation.

"What are you saying, Miss Cleaver?" she exclaimed, sharply. "Is this the way you keep your promise to me. You told me you would not repeat this . . . this nonsense to anyone else. If you have . . . hallucinations, you need not try to frighten other people. I am really surprised at you."

Susan Cleaver began to sob. Peggy administered her restorative and said no more. Cook opened her mouth to speak and then, thinking better of it, went into the scullery. After a violent effort of self-control, Susan gave a gulp and besought Peggy's forgiveness.

"I am really ashamed of myself," she pleaded, "after all your kindness. I don't now what came over me. I hardly knew what I was saying. Please do forgive me, Mrs. Dacre, for breaking my word. I'm subject to these . . . these spasms and . . . queer fancies. I sometimes think I'm going out of my mind with trouble and misery—I do indeed (sob). You've been so good to me—I wouldn't vex you for anything. Do, *do* forgive me."

"Of course I do. I spoke hastily," said Peggy, laying a hand on her shoulder kindly. "After what you've been through, I don't wonder you get a little distraught and fancy strange things sometimes. Now we're all going to have tea and play with the children till bed-time. It's past five o'clock and Billikin is getting tired, after such an exciting day. I wonder if you'll mind helping to clear up the mess in the drawing-room while we're at tea. Or don't you feel well enough?"

The colour, which had begun to tint faintly the woman's white cheeks, deepened as she replied with a hesitating stammer:

"Would you think m-me very rude . . . and—ungrateful, if I went home now?" she said. "You know I should like to help . . . in any way I could, but . . . but I am feeling so—shaky—I think I had better go."

Peggy, who felt that her going would be a relief, for she feared lest the maids should question her further, gladly consented. She was looking at the table, spread for tea in the morning-room, and lighting little candles on the Christmas cake, when Susan stole in and shut the door behind her. She was in her coat and hat ready to depart.

"I've told the girls not to believe anything I said, or the children said, about . . . you know what, ma'am," she half-whispered. "I've said it's the poor light and shadows that cause such fancies. But *you* know, ma'am, it wasn't fancy. You know what I saw."

"Yes, I know," Peggy's voice trembled a little. "But if the girls think this house is haunted they won't stay here. You see how I am fixed. It is most awkward. I wish, from my heart, we had never come."

"I don't wonder at that. But I am sure they won't leave you ma'am. Those girls are so fond of you, and the children. And they know when they are well off. Don't you be afraid of that, my dear. They're not so silly as that."

"Well, I hope you're right. But one never knows. Panic makes people do strange things."

She paused, and then asked, as Susan was turning towards the door:

"You are quite sure you saw him, Miss Cleaver? It wasn't a shadow—or anything? I could see nothing."

"No: it wasn't any shadow. There he stood by the door, smiling, like I've seen him a hundred times, one hand in his pocket and the other fumbling his watch-chain. It seemed for the moment as if I was back in the past and should hear him say—like he used—'Is my tea ready, Susan?' I almost did hear him. And then it all rushed back over me that he was dead and buried. Oh, my poor Master—my poor, dear kind Master, cut off before . . . "

"Don't!" cried Peggy, shuddering. "You make me creep. I've got to live in this house, remember. It's all very well for you, who don't. But if it goes on, I can't live here—*I won't*. It will drive me crazy! Something must be done."

She found herself now trembling all over and on the verge of tears. A shout of elfin laughter from the drawing-room acted as a tonic and she pulled herself together. The old belief returned in force, that the children could protect and comfort her in all ills. At the sound of their merriment she drew a long breath of relief and smiled.

"Hark at them!" she said. "Their Daddy is sending them into fits of laughter."

"God bless them—and bless you all," Susan Cleaver uttered, brokenly. "For all your goodness to me, I cannot ever thank you enough. You deserve to be happy if anyone does, my dear. God bless you! Good night."

She went out, and there was something in the droop of her shoulders and her lagging step that suggested age and despair. She was not an old woman; probably not much over fifty; yet Peggy realized that the fire and energy of youth, and even of middle age, had left her; that her heart was broken. And the broken heart, though it may go on beating for many years, does not keep the spirit young, the muscles strong, the vitality fresh. She could have shed a tear, then, for Susan Cleaver.

But she shook off all unhappy thoughts and, after a last glance at the pretty, bright table, went to fetch her darlings to tea.

CHAPTER XIX

AFTER the children had gone to bed and the mess of paper and rubbish had been cleared from the drawing-room, Peggy and her husband sat down by the fire and drew breath. The dismantled tree stood in a corner, like the ghost of a departed joy; a north-west wind moaned in the chimney and whistled in the keyhole. There was not much sound from the nursery upstairs, for the children were very tired. The two babies had gone to sleep the moment their heads touched the pillows, and the elder ones were not as rumbustical as usual. Peggy was indulging in her first cigarette that day and Percy sucked a beloved and comforting pipe.

"Ugh!" said Peggy, with a little shiver. "Doesn't it sound eerie to-night? I hate this nor-wester, Perks. It always seems so unhappy, somehow, like a lost spirit wailing about the house."

"I rather like it," he said. "It gives me a comfortable sort of feeling to hear the wind outside—any sort of wind—to think I'm out of it."

"And I hate any sort of wind," was Peggy's response. "It always makes me feel melancholy and depressed, but this is the worst of all. Hear how it whines and wails!"

Percy smiled. "Only in the imagination of my Bosom's Pride," he said. "She alone hears the whines and wails. I hear nothing but jolly little whistles and dancing raindrops on the window-pane."

There was a pause.

"I'm sure the imps thoroughly enjoyed their Christmas," then said Peggy, looking into the fire with a tender smile on her lips, and a loving thought went upstairs in the smoke of her cigarette.

"The tree was a great success, wasn't it?"

"Immense. It has all been a success except that wretched woman. She very nearly spoilt it all. Can't think what made you ask her."

"I am sorry for her."

"You can't be a Fairy Godmother to everyone you are sorry for, my Cherubic Angel; it's a flat impossibility. Confess now, you're sorry you asked her."

"I'm not. I couldn't have enjoyed myself thinking of her all alone and unhappy at Christmas time. Of course I can't be a Fairy Godmother to everyone, but luckily I don't know any other lonely and unhappy people at this moment."

"You don't seem to realize, Peg-o'-my-Heart, that lots of people enjoy being unhappy. They hug and cultivate their miseries instead of trying to forget them. I should say that the fair Susan is one of these. I only hope she has not upset the apple-cart in this 'appy 'ome. The maids looked scared to death."

Peggy did not reply immediately. She could not deny Percy's statement that the maids had been scared, especially after overhearing Susan's words to Cookie. And had she not been as scared herself—even more scared? For her own fears were doubled. The fear of having to visit registry offices is no light matter to a house-mistress![11]

"Percy," she said at last, "I want you to listen seriously to what I have to say, and not scoff as you always do. For this matter is a graver one than you seem to think. It is all very well to be as

[11] Registry offices were the equivalent of modern employment agencies. The mistress of a house would contact a registry office with her requirements, and she would pay a fee to have those matched with a suitable servant who was looking for a position.

cocksure as you are about everything on earth and in heaven, and to reject every theory that doesn't fit in with your fixed idea of a scheme of things. But, whether you like it or not, whether you believe it or not, this house *is* haunted. Susan Cleaver saw that old man as plainly as I see you now."

"So she says, no doubt."

"She is a decent, truthful soul; why should she lie to me? Why should all the colour go from her face, just when she is happy and laughing with the children? Do be reasonable, Percy, and give other people credit for the honesty and truthfulness you credit yourself with."

"I don't say the woman's untruthful. But she only saw what she wanted to see—what she, probably, tried to see."

Peggy gave a little gesture of impatience.

"Percy, don't you know that there are plenty of people to-day—men as intelligent and even cleverer than yourself—who believe that there does exist a more attenuated form of matter than that of which our bodies are composed; and that this etheric matter—or whatever they call it, clothes the spirit when it is free from the flesh? Do you not realize that, all through the ages, and no less to-day, men have believed in the gift of second sight, which is the power, possessed by the few, of seeing what is invisible to the many?"

"My poppet, some people will believe anything."

"And some people will believe nothing they can't touch!" she retorted. "I am speaking of men like Sir Oliver Lodge, and Flammarion—not weak credulous fools, but men of great intellect and scientific vision. How do you account for their deliberate, written statements and challenge to the world?"

"I don't account for it. I am a poor, grovelling worm, I know. But their testimony always appears to me very thin stuff."

"Because you *wish* to think so. Grant, at least, that they are honest and their brains are not addled; that it is quite possible they may be right and you wrong."

"Certainly, I grant it. I am not such a fool as to think my verdict on any subject is final. They may have had some convincing experience that I haven't. All I say is, my Precious Pegtop, that until I *have* had that experience, I can't believe that spirits hang about this earth, after they have left their bodies, to scare people and get inside the skins of ignorant and illiterate mediums; to play all the silly pranks of the table-turning séances one reads of. I can't see why they should. I know I shouldn't want to, if I were a disembodied spirit."

There was a pause.

"Suppose," Peggy said then, in a low and wavering voice, "suppose you were called away from us, Percy, wouldn't you like to get in touch with me and your children, somehow—anyhow?"

"Lord, no!" he exclaimed vehemently. "I hope I'm not such a selfish oaf as to upset and frighten you like that. God forbid! What would be the good? We couldn't touch each other, or help each other, or enjoy any fun together. The only decent thing I could do would be to efface myself as quickly as possible from your mind and hope you would soon forget me, in your world of live people."

At this, Peggy began, softly, to weep.

"As if I could ever forget you!" she sobbed. "You do say dreadful things, Percy."

"Not dreadful at all," he declared, stoutly. "It is you who are dreadfully morbid, Peg. So far as I can see there is a great gulf fixed between the dead and the living, and it is a jolly good thing there is. Anyhow, I am quite sure that if I were—among the shades—

I shouldn't want to hover about my children or see them at all. It would be hellish torture! And when I hear women sing that sentimental song about the dead mother haunting the nursery at night, I want to howl them down! Can't you realize what the mother's feelings would be? Or what kind of mother she would be who tried to harrow her children's feelings so? No, my dear child; this world of ours has troubles enough. Let us pray they don't extend to the next."

Peggy wiped her eyes. "We shall feel very differently about such things, I expect," she murmured. "The child supposed to be singing the song isn't harrowed or frightened. And perhaps the mother wouldn't be 'tortured,' as you think."

"Well, let us hope not. I must confess all such sickly and morbid songs, and stories, leave me very cold—and rather irritable. I'm afraid I'm rather a beast. But you ought to know my limits by now, old lady, and they ought not to surprise you."

"They don't," she laughed through tears, "but when you talk of being among the shadows—I . . . "

The handkerchief was requisitioned again.

"I talk, *I!*" he cried. "Why, it was *you* started it, you little minx! Didn't you . . . " he paused, put his pipe down on the ash-tray and went to sit on the arm of her chair. "Aren't you a horrid little hussy, to go on like this to your poor Perks and shed tears on a Christmas night? Aren't you now?" he demanded, putting an arm round her neck and turning up her face, on which tears shone, to his own.

"Yes, I am," bleated Peggy, "I'm a rotten little silly superstitious donkey, but I can't help it."

"Of course you can't. That accursed old Fairy Godmother who wasn't invited to your christening, inflicted on you that worst of evils, a tender heart. Result: you go inviting stray spinsters to share your festivities and the S. S. upsets the whole show. Too bad! Why can't you have a flinty, tough, and desiccated old heart like your loving spouse's?"

There was a short interval of endearments, over which a veil may be drawn, and when Percy had gone back to his pipe, Peggy said:

"You're a dreadful canoodler, Perks, a positive Lovelace—and no woman is safe from you.[12] But I've got to stand up against you, whatever you say, for the Wife of your Bosom is no doormat to be walked over."

"As if I didn't know that, Tyrant!" he murmured.

"And what I have to say, and will say, is that this question must be faced. Are things normal in this house? It is all very well to blame the poor spinster, Susan Cleaver, for upsetting us, but I've been upset before I ever saw Susan Cleaver, and you know it. I knew there was something wrong from the first. Because you don't feel this, or see, or hear anything, you are prepared to laugh at our fears, to accuse me, and Susan Cleaver and the children—yes—and even Joan Millis—of being credulous fools, the victims of our heated imaginations. We've all seen and heard things. Gib and K. have seen a shape solid enough to make them think it a real man. It may be only an 'impalpable impression on the air,' it may be subjective and not objective; some vision formed in our minds; but there is *something*—something to cause the vision, to project it outside of us. What is it? Why have the children talked about 'the old man in the garden'? Why did Gib and K. see him last night, and Susan Cleaver again to-night? We were all jolly and matter-of-fact enough; nobody was thinking of ghosts or hauntings.

---

[12] Lovelace: an elegant seducer of women.

Why was that woman petrified with fear? Why?"

"I'm blowed if I know," said Percy.

He was silent about a minute, and then added thoughtfully: "I will frankly admit, Peg, that there's something I don't understand about it all."

"There's my sensible Perks! That's all I wanted to hear from you. Do you know, darling, there are times when I really like you, and this is one of them."

"I've sometimes suspected it," he said, and they chuckled a little together. She looked at him, sitting in the chair opposite, at the kink in his hair, the twinkle in his eyes, the thin, strong, capable hands, and thought: "He's quite the biggest darling in the whole world and I adore every inch of him."

Aloud she said: "Yes, you are not at all a bad sort—at times—Perks, in fact, I believe there are many worse, only they keep 'em locked up. But to return to our subject. Having got so far as to admit that there is something queer about this house—something you cannot account for and do not understand, the next question is—what are we to do about it?"

"Dashed if I know. We can't clear out. There isn't another house in the land to be had for the same price, and I can't afford another move so soon. We've got to stick it, my Angel Bird . . . I suppose one can get used to anything."

"Not to . . . ghosts." She lowered her voice and glanced over her shoulders. "No, Perks, I can't do that, and I'm not going to try. One never knows how soon these . . . these manifestations may terrify the children, or the maids. I won't stick it. Either I leave this house or get to the bottom of the mystery."

"How do you propose to set about it?"

"I shall write to the Society for Psychical Research and ask them to send some one down to investigate."

"Oh Lord!" he groaned. "Don't let's have any long-haired ones here, Peg, I pray and beseech you. I prefer spooks."

It was a rooted conviction of Percy Dacre's that all those he designated 'cranks' and 'faddists'—all spiritualists, communists, teetotallers, food-reformers, and reformers generally, wore their hair long. You could never argue him out of this belief.

"You prefer spooks because you're too obtuse to see or hear them," she retorted. "But we can't leave things as they are. Either I write to that Society or get a medium down."

"Worse and worse!" he groaned again. "What good would that do?"

"Find out if there is some one haunting the house, and if so, what it wants."

"My child, my poor, innocent, deluded child, are you going to believe any tale that a long-haired medium in a trance tells you? Because if you are, I'm *not*."

"Then what *do* you suggest?"

"I suggest going to bed and putting ourselves in trances. Who knows if we could not thus elucidate the mystery—eh? What?"

Peggy gave a long sigh of impatience and exasperation.

"You are the limit!" she said.

"I'm inclined to believe you, my love," he said, yawning. "But the fact of the matter is, I find the old-fashioned Christmas vastly exhausting. I don't know which is most tired, my legs, my mind, or my jaws. I feel as if I'd been up two days and eaten ten meals. Why do we always over-eat at Christmas? Come, my Poppet, let's to bed."

They went, and Peggy, worn out with her strenuous day, was just dropping off to sleep when a voice from the other bed roused her, and she heard Percy say:

"You asleep, Peg? I'm illuminated with a most brilliant idea!"

"What is it?" she asked, drowsily.

"Ever heard me speak of a chap named Fabian Keary? I used to know him rather well at one time, but have lost sight of him lately."

"I don't remember the name. What about him?"

"He was a sort of—I don't know what you call 'em—but he boasted of second sight and had weird visions. Irish by birth, with a banshee in the family—and all that. We used to rag him about it and play tricks on him, but he never turned a hair, and sometimes he got his own back. He was a 'psychic' as they make 'em! He could tell what you were thinking about—or guessed it—and he used to swear he could see 'auras' floating round us. But he was quite a jolly oaf, nevertheless, and we all liked him at the Art School. He couldn't paint for nuts, and didn't even think he could, but he worked as hard as any of us, never missed a class. I have an idea he went into an architect's office. If I can find out where he is now, I'll ask him down. He'll rout out that spook, if anyone can."

Peggy became enthusiastic.

"The very thing!" she cried, now wide-awake. "But supposing he has gone away—to Canada or somewhere? He may be at the other side of the world by now. When did you see him last? Now I come to think of it I seem to have some faint recollection about him; but I forgot what it was about."

"I expect it was about his saving me from an untimely grave."

"Oh, that was the man! Yes, I remember. But tell me the details again."

"I was going up to Scotland by the night express. We'd had lunch together, Keary and two or three others. I went back to my digs, and had packed my tooth-brush and was just having a final meal about seven, when in rushed Keary and said: 'You can't go by that train Dacre. It isn't safe.' Of course I only laughed at him, as we always did at his fancies, but the more I laughed the more earnest he got. He had *seen* a railway accident, he said, in one of his queer visions, and I was in it."

"And so you had the sense not to go by that train."

"My precious Poppet! How well she knows her Perks! Of course I went, I am not such a feeble ass as to alter my arrangements because a son of Hibernia has a vision."[13]

"But was there an accident?"

"Yes, there was an accident all right. But I wasn't killed, as you might observe. As a concession to his pleading I promised to travel in the back part of the train, and, as it happened my coach was left only swinging off the rails, not smashed up. It wasn't a nice experience; I was pitched on the man opposite and nearly broke his nose. I've a very distinct recollection of his language, which was 'painful and free.' But the first carriages were all splintered to ribbons. It was a horrible business. I helped with the stretchers."

"And yet you don't believe in occult influence. You won't admit you owe your life to Keary's second sight."

"I didn't say that. To tell the truth, I was impressed at the time and I'm not prepared to deny there might be something in it. But there are such things as coincidences, my child. I can never see how anyone can ever know what is *going* to happen. A hundred things may prevent it. And if we believe that all occurrences are planned out beforehand, what becomes of personal will and direction? It seems to me such a belief would absolutely paralyse resolution, and we should have no more say in our own actions, or in our future,

---

[13] Hibernia: the classical Latin name for Ireland.

than if we were potatoes! No. I'm not of the Calvinistic persuasion at all, and have no faith in predestination."

"What did you say to Keary?" asked Peggy, who was in no mood for argument.

"I sent him a wire saying: 'All right. One up to you.' Of course the next time we met he crowed extensively, and expected me to fall on his neck for having saved my life."

"And didn't you?"

"I did not. But I stood him a drink. Which may be as much as I am worth."

"We'll have him here," declared Peggy, resolutely. "That is, if he is to be found. Oh, I *am* glad you thought of him, Perks! How shall you set about finding him?"

"I shall write to his Club. He used to be a member of the Vagabonds. He may not be now, as he was given to changes and probably chucked it for another. But I can try."

"You'll write in the morning, won't you? You won't put it off."

"I will write first thing after breakfast, O Moon of my Desire. You may depend on me. Goo'-ni'."

He was soon asleep. Not so Peggy, who churned over her thoughts for a long while and heard the neighbouring cocks stab the darkness at three o'clock.

CHAPTER XX

PERCY wrote to Fabian Keary, as he promised, next morning.

"Dear Keary," he said, "Are you still in the flesh? If you are, and this reaches you, will you run down here and try to rout out a spook who is roosting in this house and worrying my wife into fits? I haven't seen or heard anything of it myself, but she has—or thinks she has—and the scare is spreading. I recall your uncanny powers and am sure that you will be able to ferret out the cause of the trouble, if anyone can. Any old time will suit us.

"Yours,

"P. M. DACRE."

He did not have any reply for a few days, and then Keary wrote:

"DEAR DACRE,

"I was more than pleased to hear from you again and shall be delighted to run down and see you next Friday, if that will suit Mrs. D. I only got your letter last night, when I returned from a visit to Erin. Glad you attribute 'uncanny powers' to me. It looks like a change of heart and recantation of scepticism! I've always told you there were more things in heaven and earth than were dreamt of in your philosophy; but I won't promise to 'rout the spook' who is haunting you. For that I possess no qualifications. All I might be able to do is to discover whether there is any discarnate entity in your house and, if so, of what nature it is. My respects to your wife and thanks for her invitation.

"Yours,

"F. KEARY."

Percy had qualms when he read the words "discarnate entity," and, from the tenor of the letter, realized that he had capitulated so far as to admit there was something in his house answering to that unpleasant description. He was not disposed to put any faith in things "discarnate" which Keary evidently took as a matter of course, and he began to ask himself what effect his Irish friend would have upon Peggy. Had he not been rash to invite such an uncanny person to pay them a visit? Doubt, as we know, invites doubt. Percy recalled many past traits in Keary; how he was erratic and changeable, occasionally wild in his talk, careless in his dress and odd in his ways. By now he might be quite unpresentable, and shock, not only Peggy, but the decorous country town in which they lived. Suppose Keary turned up with a half-grown beard, no collar and queer clothes! It was quite on the cards that he might. Suppose Peggy found him detestable and the children were afraid of him! Suppose, once here, he wouldn't go!

These nightmarish surmises flitted through Percy's mind when he had read the letter, and the worst of them was that he might not be able to get rid of Keary if they didn't like him. Why on earth hadn't he asked the fellow for a definite period—say, "a week-end," or "a night or two"? Instead of that he had asked him merely to come down and "rout a spook." Now it might take a month to rout a spook, or Keary might say so, if he wanted free lodgings for that period. Possibly he was hard up, as he always used to be, having an incurable tendency to spend more than his income. And if he found The Beeches comfortable he would stay there. Percy knew himself and Peggy well enough to be aware than any visitor would stay just as long as he liked; neither of them would ever have the courage even to hint at his departure. They were two pitiable cowards in that respect.

The only thing that reassured him was Keary's address, which seemed to indicate that he was doing well in his profession, and not likely to have too much time on his hands. Anyhow, the deed was done, the invitation had been sent and accepted. There was nothing for it now but to wait and see what sort of a spirit he had invoked.

Peggy was quite excited at the prospect of entertaining Keary, and Percy kept his fears to himself. He did indeed warn her that Keary might not be quite what she expected to see; that he was naturally unconventional and might wear strange ties and socks and collars. He was almost certain to have long hair, and might not even clean his nails! Percy thought that quite possible. But these alarming suggestions had no effect on Peggy. She declared a weakness for unconventional people, and had no prejudice against long hair, as Percy had. The more odd Keary was in appearance, the more different from other people, the more likely, she argued, he would be to exorcise the haunting spirit in the house. Percy could not follow the logic of this; but he said no more and awaited his guest in some trepidation.

His fears, however, vanished when he met Keary at the station. He looked perfectly respectable, far more so than when Percy had last seen him, and had the unmistakable air of a prosperous gentleman. He was wearing a well-cut overcoat and carried a small leather suitcase that did not suggest more than a week-end visit. A smallish man, with light hair a trifle long, according to Percy's standard, and deep-set, dreamy eyes; he had a keen, clever face, and prepossessed manner. In his speech was only the faintest suspicion of a brogue, and he had a frank, winning smile.

The children took to him at once and were all over him, which convinced Peggy of his extreme worth. She had a slight shock, not unmixed with disappointment, when he announced that he was a vegetarian, having prepared rather a choice menu for his dinner; but he reassured her by declaring that he could always enjoy a meal of potatoes, bread, and cheese, and asked nothing better in the way of a repast. In spite of her chagrin at seeing her soup, fish, and fowl declined, she saw with pleasure his hearty appetite for vegetables, sweets, and fruit, and even began to wonder if she could not do without meat herself and save on her butcher's bills.

"Now about this spook," said Keary, when they were having coffee in the drawing-room. "Did you know the house was haunted when you took it?"

The subject had not been broached at dinner. Both Peggy and her husband felt a little shy of it.

"I'm not prepared to admit the haunting," said Percy, smiling. "The cigs, are by your side, Keary. Help yourself."

"You said there was a spook," Keary reminded him, taking another cigarette.

"No, I said it was my wife's idea."

"Then I address myself to Mrs. Dacre, and should like to hear her idea. May I remind you, old man, that such ideas do not arise out of nothing at all. You don't suppose it 'growed,' like Topsy, do you?"[14]

"Why not? Ideas do grow out of nothing. I know mine do. I sit before a sheet of cartridge paper, often, with my mind blank, until something pops into it."

"Up from below," remarked Keary, "sent up by the subconscious self. Of course we all know that. The theory of auto-suggestion

---

[14] Topsy is a character from *Uncle Tom's Cabin* by Harriet Beecher Stowe. On the subject of God, when asked 'Do you know who made you?', Topsy replies, 'I spect I grow'd.'

is well-established now. But in that case you are definitely seeking ideas. Mrs. Dacre, if I am not mistaken, had no desire to encounter any manifestation from the unseen world, and it is therefore unlikely that auto-suggestion had anything to do with what she saw or heard. May I hear all about it, Mrs. Dacre, and have I your permission to squash Percy if he chips in?"

"You certainly have," said Peggy, laughing, "that is, if you can. It's not easy to squash Percy, I assure you. He is the most doubting of Thomases, Mr. Keary, and believes in nothing that he can't see, hear, or feel."

"Poor earthworm! How does he account for all the wonders and mysteries surrounding us, clues to which are being discovered day by day, on the psychic plane?"

"I don't pretend to account for anything. I simply question and wait," said Percy. "If you can satisfy my reason . . . "

"Reason!" interrupted Keary, with superb scorn. "What is reason? It generally means arguing round in a circle, tethered to a peg, like a goat in a field, the peg of your own mental bias! Our reasoning faculties are really only of value to us, as the dog's nose is to the dog, for the purpose of snuffing out things hidden and following trails; but most people seem to think they are merely scales for weighing. 'I trust my reason,' you hear people say, and their reason sways them on the side that their inherited prejudices are weighted."

Percy coughed, significantly.

"Yes, I know," Keary laughed. "Hitting at you, old man. Well, if the cap fits, why not wear it? You use your reason to make everything square to your own ideas. Marconi used his to discover the hidden laws governing sound-waves. Others have used theirs to discover other laws relating to etheric bodies, invisible to most of us, but just as demonstrable as the wireless when once mastered. Why should you, man, have the arrogance to suppose that your gross body, fed on the carcasses of other animals, is composed of the only kind of matter there is in the universe?"

This sent Percy off into a delighted roar of laughter. Keary was a crank, he thought, but a most amusing crank. And Percy's laugh was the most infectious in the world. The others joined in, but Keary's eyes were earnest.

" 'What is mind? No matter. What is matter? Never mind,' " Percy quoted.[15] "But I can assure you, Keary, it is not the feeding of my vile body on gross carcasses that makes me impervious to spooks; because the dainty and etherial Wife of my Bosom does likewise and sees 'em."

"Her spirit is not in the grip of fixed ideas," retorted Keary. "But now, will you kindly hold your peace, Dacre, while she tells me what has actually been seen and heard in this house."

Peggy told him everything, and Percy did not interrupt once. She told first about old Barker's reputation for singularity, his promise to Susan Cleaver, his failure to make a will; then went on to relate how the children had seen an old man in the garden who sat and smiled at them, but disappeared when they went to touch him. She told him of the barking dogs, the noises in the house, and finally of Susan Cleaver's fright on Christmas night.

Keary listened intently, giving a slight nod now and then, as if to show it was what he expected. When the recital was finished he turned to Percy.

"Isn't that evidence enough for you?" he asked. "What do you say to it? Have you any theory to account for these things?"

---

15 A quote from *Punch*, 'A Short Cut to Metaphysics', 14 July 1855 p. 19.

"Not a pip! Have you?"

"Certainly I have."

"Let's hear it."

"It is not a theory, but a well authenticated-truth. There can be no doubt whatever that the house is haunted. I should have known it even without your letter, or hearing this story, the moment I entered the house."

"Do you mean you could smell it, like mice?" asked Percy, with a grin.

"No, but I felt it. I sensed the evil thing as soon as my foot crossed the threshold."

His words gave a sudden shock to both his hearers. They had not expected anything like this.

"Evil thing!" cried Peggy, in alarm. "What do you mean by that, Mr. Keary? Why 'evil'?"

"Just what I say, Mrs. Dacre. I don't know why, but there is certainly some mischievous agency at work here, some malign intelligence. We call such intelligences 'Elementals.' They can be dangerous. I give you fair warning, not to let the thing go on too long."

"Oh, gosh!" Percy exclaimed impatiently. "What are you handing us, Keary? It's not good enough. You don't expect me to believe that tosh?"

He was now seriously annoyed, and wished heartily that he had not invited Keary to come. Obviously the man was frightening Peggy even more than she was frightened before. Her eyes were dilated with fear.

"No doubt," returned Keary, calmly, "it seems tosh to you. As I said before, you have not the fine perceptions necessary to a comprehension of the arcana. Things occult are, and probably always will be, a sealed book to you. That is why you have not seen or heard the manifestations of this elemental spirit who is seeking control of your wife."

"Control my wife! Good Lord, what next?" ejaculated Percy.

"It is as well to face the matter squarely, Dacre. Something has got into your house with an ill purpose, and will have to be exorcised. Something mischievous and soulless. I used the word 'evil' just now, because such entities are without a governing moral sense of conscience. They are not conspicuously wicked or immoral: they are simply, as their name implies, elemental. But they have one terribly dangerous desire; to enter into the body of a human being, and oust its soul. And when once this is achieved, when a man or woman is thus made subject to the control of an Elemental, the mischief is done. It is next to impossible to dislodge it. I have no doubt at all in my mind that such an Entity is trying to force an entrance into one of you here, probably Mrs. Darce."

"Does it think to achieve its desired end by shoving furniture about and making ridiculous noises, barking like dogs and so forth?"

"As I said before, these Elementals are undeveloped childish intelligences; therefore liable to do childish and silly things," said Keary. "I suppose they have a vague idea of terrifying people out of their senses, and then, when the soul is thus driven out, taking its place."

Percy raised his eyes to heaven.

"Of all the crazy nonsense I ever heard——" he began; but Peggy stopped him.

"If it is an Elemental who is here, why have the children seen an old man?" she queried.

"They often take the shape of dead persons when they materialize," was the glib reply. "It is a very common thing, let me assure you, Mrs. Dacre, for people to see their loved ones at séances.

But they are deluded. I accepted your invitation to come here because I felt sure that I could help you to 'rout the spook' as Percy called it. And that can only be done by exorcism. You must not attempt to deal with this unholy thing in any other way. Believe me, it is dangerous to meddle ignorantly in these matters. I've been through it, so I ought to know."

His face grew deadly earnest, so earnest that Peggy grew paler even than before, and Percy ceased to scoff. You cannot scoff at a man's beliefs when you see that they are held with genuine and passionate conviction.

"Some years ago," Keary went on, "I dabbled in spiritualism. I went to a number of séances and had extraordinary experiences. Presently I began to find that I was under control by something outside myself, something that made me do strange things against my own will. And a man I knew well lost himself—his volition and command—altogether. He became literally, in the old Biblical sense 'possessed of devils,' and finally dared not move without having another human being on either side of him, for he declared that there were grinning demons all around him, ready to pounce. It was dreadful to see the poor chap, and, at last, he died, quite mad. At least, that was the medical verdict. I think myself, and others thought too, that if he had been properly exorcised the evil Control might have been routed. But his people were sceptical, and only laughed at the idea of demonic possession."

Peggy shivered and drew her chair nearer the fire.

"Do you really believe in it?" she asked, "and in exorcism?"

"As I believe in God and the Author of Evil. The Church teaches it, has always taught it. Can you read your Bible and doubt it? We laugh—that is—many people laugh to-day at the old belief in witchcraft. What of the Witch of Endor? And there are witches to-day, as there ever have been, persons who traffic with evil and worship it. When black magic was stamped out, perhaps with unnecessary cruelty, it was an untold benefit to mankind; saving millions of souls from perdition. For it was spreading through Europe, like a hideous disease and becoming a fearful menace to religion and morality."

"You are a Roman Catholic, Keary, aren't you?" asked Percy, abruptly.

"I am. It was a Catholic who saved me, and I have been one ever since. Of course it was the faith of my fathers; but I had lapsed from it, and so became an easy prey to those who lie in wait for human souls."

Peggy recalled suddenly a certain sign made by Keary as he came into the house, which had puzzled her a little. Now she understood. It was the Sign of the Cross.

Both she and Percy were stricken into silence for some minutes, feeling perturbed and uncomfortable.

"Then you don't believe that . . . Thing that haunts this house is old Barker?" said Peggy then.

"Certainly not. The dead are not permitted to return. They are in Heaven or Purgatory. All these tales of spiritualists who see and converse with their departed ones are delusions. I ask you—are the records of such visitations convincing? Can any sensible person read accounts of Planchette; table-turning; musical instruments and hands, floating about in the air, childish messages and so forth without scepticism? Is it likely that spirits purged of all earthly grossness could behave so? No. All such manifestations are obviously the sport of elemental intelligences that may, at any moment, become a menacing evil."

"I don't believe one bally word of it, or of what you say about devils either," exclaimed Percy, with sudden ferocity. "My religion, what there is of it, reposes on the eternal power and goodness of God, the Father of us all, and Ruler of all things. He would have no truck with spooks and devils."

Peggy had never seen her husband like this before, although she knew him to be more deeply religious at heart than he ever professed to be. It was a new Percy to her who rose now and began to make up the fire with nervous energy. She could see that he was perturbed and angry, but did not guess that it was chiefly on her account. He saw the impression Keary was making on her plastic mind, and feared it.

"Don't you believe that there is also an Evil Principle at war with Eternal Goodness?" demanded Keary. "Whether you do or not, you are certainly up against it now, in one of its myriad forms. And you will have no peace until it is driven out of this house by exorcism. I knew a man in the same case. Terrible things happened in his home. He was nearly killed, once by a heavy picture falling quite close to his head, and another time by a chimney-stack. Windows were thrown wide-open in the night; all the lights would go out suddenly, and so forth. But after a priest had gone through the house, using the orthodox form of exorcism in each room, the hauntings ceased. I would advise you to have that done here."

Peggy recalled Joan's story.

"I wonder if we could——" she began; but Percy turned on her fiercely.

"We certainly shall *not.* I'll have no priest doing his mumbo-jumbo, with 'bell, book, and candle,' in my house. It is time we shook off all that mediæval superstition. I don't want to be rude to you Keary, but you must excuse me if I say that all this sounds to me like damn tomfoolery. I can't help your beliefs—I have no desire to change them. Each man's religion is his own affair. But I wish you hadn't tried to stuff up my wife's head with your—to me—crazy notions; and I hope to hear no more of them. She is highly nervous and your words will haunt her worse than any spook could do."

A dark flush rose to Keary's face and his eyes flashed. All his Irish blood was instantly up to meet affront.

"In that case, the sooner I depart the better," he exclaimed, rising.

"No, no," cried Peggy, seizing him by the coat. "Sit down, Mr. Keary, and don't be offended with Perks. You see how prejudiced and sceptical he is; but he can't help it, poor dear! He didn't mean to insult you. And I'm *not* highly nervous—that's only his idea. Please, *please*, don't be vexed. We are most grateful to you for coming, and for your advice."

Keary was instantly placated and looked into her pleading eyes with a frank and kindly smile.

"I know—I quite understand," he said. "The Protestant mind is like that, and Dacre is a true-born, stubborn Englishmen, as I am a true-born Irishman. I can't expect him to see things as I do. And I'm not going to say another word on the subject. I've said all there is to say. I've given you my candid opinion about your ghost and can do nothing more in the matter."

"Good old Keary! We'll have a drink now and drown our differences in the flowing bowl," said Percy. "I grovel before you and humbly apologize for my improper behaviour towards a guest. You see the sort of cub I am and what my poor downtrodden spouse has to put up with."

"It is awful to have to live under a tyrant!" Peggy agreed.

"You have my sympathy," said Keary, gravely. "I have a temper of my own."

"Glad you told us, old chap," said Percy. "Say when." He held up a decanter.

The rest of the evening passed pleasantly enough, and next day Keary left them, urging an appointment in town. But they both believed he had intended to stay for the week-end, and Percy, at least, inwardly commended his wisdom in not doing so. He drew a breath of relief when the visitor had gone.

CHAPTER XXI

THE visit of Fabian Keary, it will be seen, was more than a disappointment; it increased the trouble that it had been intended to remove. For all his pleasantness, he left a very unpleasant impression behind him, a sense of new horror and disaster. Percy, of course, would not admit this and laughed at his warnings as "unutterable nonsense," but Keary had, nevertheless, succeeded in making him feel thoroughly uncomfortable. It does not matter how sceptical a man may be; he cannot be told that his house harbours devils without having disagreeable sensations. The "something evil" under his roof caught Percy's imagination and festered in his mind like a bad germ. And he was angry with the man for frightening Peggy. While she had believed in the phantasm of old Barker, she had been scared enough, but not desperately afraid, as she now was. It was indeed a terribly devastating thought that a devil—even a merely elemental devil—was lying in wait for one, ready to take possession of one's soul, or the soul of one near and dear. Keary had filled her mind with fresh terror, which she could not conceal.

"It is all very well to laugh, Percy," she said, "but all Mr. Keary said was quite reasonable . . . and . . . scientific. It sounded true, and he was so positive about it. He spoke as if he really *knew*."

"The less people know, the more positive they are," said Percy.

"Nobody could be more positive than you are, Perks, against all spiritual manifestations," she retorted.

"Just what I say. Because I know nothing about them. Keary's positive for the same reason."

"Don't quibble. Mr. Keary has studied this matter and does know something about it. Besides, he has the Church behind him—and the Bible. We read of demonic possession there."

Percy groaned, seized his head with both hands, and pretended to tear his hair.

"Oh, Mistress Mine, how you do try me!" he exclaimed. "It is a punishment for my sins. Why did I ever ask the fool here? I might have foreseen he would fill your simple mind with tommy-rot. I begin to fear you are possessed already, or you wouldn't torment your devoted slave as you do. When it comes to hurling the Bible at him——"

Peggy broke in: "Percy, do be serious a minute. What shall we do next? May I write to the Society for Psychical Research and ask if they think there is anything in what Mr. Keary said?"

"If you do, the whole long-haired lot will want to land down on us and stalk our spook. I might have known what Keary was as soon as I saw his hair!"

"Don't be silly. Of course they wouldn't come unless I invited them. And I shouldn't do that, I only want to ask their views about demonic possession. Do let me. If they denied it, or thought it a subject for doubt, it would reassure me. But this suggestion of devils, or elementals, trying to get into our bodies, or the bodies of our darling kiddies, terrifies me to pieces. I can't get it out of my head—I can't really, Perks."

Her voice had a little crack in it that went to his heart. She was standing by the fire near. He grabbed her dress and pulled her down on his knees.

"Bless the little innocent baby, was she terrified then? As if her faithful Perks wouldn't fight all the devils in hell for her! Funny, when you come to think of it, that this place was called 'Hell

Corner' before we came. You shall write to anyone you please, my Lump of Delight, if it will give you any comfort. Only don't—don't—as you value your unworthy slave—ask any of 'em here. Keary was enough! I don't object to old Barker in the least. He is quite a respectable and worthy spook. But I do object to having my 'umble 'ouse made a rendezvous of spiritualists, with séances in my drawing-room and long-haired psychics jabbering about what they don't understand. I'd as soon have a priest, with 'bell, book, and candle.' One would be no worse than the other."

"I only want to ask that one question," replied Peggy, to this tirade. "No one need come. I shan't invite investigation. I may wrote, Perks?"

"Do whatever you bally well like, my Angel."

"Have you the address in any of your books?"

The address of the Psychical Society was found, after some searching, and Peggy wrote her letter. It took her some time as she wished it to be clear and concise, and she had not a very methodical brain. There was so much matter to condense, so much to explain. It is such quick work to pour out hundreds of words in explanation; such slow work to say as much in less than half the words. When she had done her best, Peggy showed the letter to her husband, and, as he expressed approval, it was sent."

The reply did not come for several days. When it did Peggy read it with a sense of relief, but Percy was not quite so satisfied. As he expected, the Society wished to send some one down to investigate. This was the letter from the Hon. Secretary:

"DEAR MADAM,

"If, as I understand, you believe your house to be haunted by a discarnate intelligence, there can be no reason for apprehending it is evil or inimical to you in any way. Experience has shown, in thousands of instances, that such apparitions linger about the places in which their earthly life was spent. We have reason to believe that these forms can be partly intellectual, partly spiritual, and partly material; and that they are possessed, frequently, by some idea, or thought that causes their materialization. In your case it would seem to be that the spectre has an intelligent reason for manifesting itself, in that sudden death cut it off from life before a certain determined action could be fulfilled. Such a frustrated intention has often been followed by such appearances; though it is not always the cause. Indeed, it is difficult to discover why some places are perpetually haunted for no apparent reason, as they undoubtedly are, and have been for centuries.

"It is not unusual, as you suppose, for the ghost to appear to so many different persons; that is quite a common phenomenon in haunted houses; though, of course, there are certain people to whom they never become visible. The barking of dogs is a rarer manifestation that makes your case the more interesting. The reality of ultra-normal phenomena is becoming more evident every day, and is believed now to be capable of perfectly sane and scientific explanation. With a view to such an elucidation of your case, we should be very glad if you would allow the Society to send some one down to investigate the matter."

This sentence set Percy groaning. The letter went on:

"But pray disabuse your mind of any fear that the haunting is of diabolical agency. We are, it is true, surrounded by mystery and unable to maintain that the ether about is is not peopled with elemental creatures, who may, or may not, be mischievous. For that reason spiritualistic séances are not without danger, especially to weak minds. But we approach this subject in the enquiring and scientific spirit, and our long experience of haunted houses does not show that any harm has ever been wrought by apparitions. If your friend's conclusion were born out by facts, the inhabitants of all such houses would be the prey of demons and end in madness! We do not find this to be the case.

"Trusting this may reassure you, and hoping to receive your consent to an investigation, I am,

"Yours sincerely,

"J. C. MARSH."

"What did I tell you?" was Percy's comment, when Peggy had finished reading the letter to him. "Of course I knew there were no devils billeted in Hell Corner. And I knew equally well the P. S. would want to billet a long-haired one on us."

"I may ask them to send some one, mayn't I, Perks? He might set our minds at rest."

"*Our* minds! I like that. My mind is entirely at rest, thank you, ma'am. The dear old gentleman hasn't worried me at all—except by disturbing the Wife of my Bosom in such an ungentlemanly way. After all, what can the 'scientific gent.' do, if he does come down? Ten to one the spook wouldn't show up. If he didn't seize the opportunity of haunting Keary, who is psychic enough for any spook, why should he appear to this other party, who only wants to research him?"

"They might send a woman," suggested Peggy, with a sly glance at him.

"Ah, that's another matter. I should have my turn then. We could sit up and watch together, and you could go to bed, my love. I like the idea."

"Oh, you do, do you, sir?" Peggy made a face at him. "Well, I don't—unless they send a frump of mature age. But, seriously, may I ask them to send some one, Percy?"

"Do be a little gentleman, Peg, and not so vulgarly persistent. It really isn't good form to tease your poor husband like this. Haven't I hinted, as clearly as I could with delicacy, that I don't want my house invaded by spiritualists, i.e. mediums and such-like? The creature would be sure to stay a fortnight, at least. Old Barker would be far too shy to appear at once."

"Rubbish! Of course I should only invite him for a night or two."

"That is all very well. I know what you are, my Precious Poppet! He would stay just as long as he liked—as Keary would have done if he hadn't seen the glare in my eyes."

"Well, you can let the investigator see the glare in your eyes."

"He mightn't be as movable as Keary. Hang it all, Peg, an Englishman's house is his castle, and if he has a very natural objection to long-haired . . . "

A soft hand placed over his mouth stopped the flow of Percy's eloquence at this point.

"Then I understand you to say, darling, that I may invite anyone I like?" said Peggy, in her sweetest and more irresistible voice.

"Exactly. My very words! Let 'em all come. Tyrant! Why did I ever put my neck under your heel? Such a heel too! Stilt would be nearer the mark. But carry on. Do as thou wilt with thy slave. He is but a poor bread-winner and tax-payer, at the best."

"My precious Perks! There are times when I positively adore you, and this is one of them," said Peggy, with a hug.

CHAPTER XXII

PEGGY did not, however, write her letter to Mr. Marsh for some time. She shrank from the idea of inviting a perfect stranger to her house as much as Percy did, and dreaded the possibility of having to sit up all night watching for the ghost that might not appear. Some one would have to sit up, they decided, if the "investigator" desired to do so; and it seemed highly probable that he would. In all the records of such investigations of haunted houses they had ever read, whether in news columns or fiction, some one had sat up to watch for ghostly manifestations. She and Percy discussed this matter perpetually and decided that they would both watch, if necessary, as Peggy declined to be left alone in bed and could not keep "the long-haired one" company while her husband slept above. In any case she knew there would be no sleep for her, and sensed, in advance, a taut condition of nerves, ready to be terrified by a sound.

Moreover, at this time they had a number of social engagements which made it difficult to find a couple of free days and nights when they could entertain a guest. They had been invited to two dances, a dinner, and a Bridge Drive; had invited some people to dine one night, and Peggy was giving a children's party at the end of the month. She kept putting off the letter day after day, to avoid fixing a date, and now invitations for February were beginning to come in. The Dacres had jumped straight into popularity with the little circle that formed Leatheringham's select society and everybody was eager for their friendship. As the weeks slipped by Peggy found it increasingly difficult to make up her mind. She sent Mr. Marsh a few lines, acknowledging his letter and promising to write again later; but it is quite possible this promise might have been left unfulfilled if something had not occurred to pull her up with a jerk and throw her back on her first resolution.

For a month nothing had been seen or heard to cause any vibrations of fear in the household; and, as usual, Peggy began to tell herself that she had been a fanciful little fool and that all the phenomena at Christmas and before had been the work of her heated imagination. Then the thing happened again.

She and Percy were going to a dance one night, and, after an early dinner, she went upstairs to put the final touches to her toilet. Standing in front of the long glass in her room, with her hands raised to her hair, she saw something move behind her own reflection and a figure appear in the doorway opposite. At first she thought it was Percy and said: "Shan't be a minute, Perks." Then she saw that it was not Percy's face, and was suddenly frozen stiff with horror.

All the blood seemed to run from her veins and her own face in the glass became fixed and ghastly. She could neither move nor cry out. Her hands fell to her side and she stood as if petrified into stone.

The face in the glass beside her own was not more ghastly than her own. It was that of an old man; slightly bald, with a clipped beard, and his lips were set in a strange smile that belied the earnest pleading of his eyes.

Her heart began to thud in her ears, a mist clouded her eyes and she felt every bit of strength go out of her muscles. In another moment she would have fallen to the ground.

Then Percy's voice from below pulled her together. She caught her breath, moved, and steadied herself by holding on to the dressing-table.

"Hurry up, Peg!" he called. And the figure by the door vanished from the glass.

"Perks! Come here!" she cried, as loudly as she could. It was a faint enough cry, but he heard it and ran upstairs, to find her lying back in an arm-chair, white as chalk and shaking.

"Peggy! What is it? What is the matter?" he ejaculated, kneeling down by her and rubbing her icy hands.

"I've seen him," she panted, through her chattering teeth. "Oh, Perks. I'm going to faint."

"No, you're not—nonsense!"

He sprang up. She seized his hand.

"Don't leave me," she cried.

"I won't leave you." He went to the bell and rang furiously. Nanny came running up, alarmed.

"Get me the whiskey. Mrs. Dacre feels faint," he said, and the girl ran down to fulfil the order.

After a gulp of the spirit, almost neat, Peggy choked and a little pink stole back to her cheeks. Nanny, who stood watching with a frightened face, asked if she should go for a doctor.

"No, I am quite all right now, Nanny. Thank you so much," Peggy said, smiling, and the girl went down, reassured. As soon as her footsteps died away, Peggy grabbed Percy's hand again and exclaimed:

"Oh, Perks, I saw him—quite, *quite* plainly! He was standing in the doorway looking as solid and real as you are, but oh! so unutterably sad, though he was smiling. I thought I should die of fear. My heart seemed to stop. I believe I should have died, right then, if you hadn't called out."

He gazed at her silently and gravely. His usual gibe was not forthcoming. All he could say, hesitatingly, was:

"Are you sure you didn't imagine it?"

"Why should I imagine it? I was thinking only of my frock and hair when I saw something move behind me, in the glass. At first I thought it was you, and spoke to you. Then the face became distinct——Oh-h!" she shuddered and covered her eyes with her hand.

"Don't think of it any more, little dear thing. Come down to the warm room," said Percy, taking her cold hands in his and drawing her up from the chair. There was a fire in the room, but he shivered himself, for he felt a strange chill in the air. Wrapping her up in her evening cloak, he lifted her in his arms and carried her downstairs.

When she was seated in the big Chesterfield by the fire he said:

"We can't go to the bally dance to-night. We'll sit here and be cozy together, like Darby and Joan."

"Oh, Perks! And I've had a new frock on purpose."

"I know. It's a pink of a frock and you look a perfect pink in it—or did, till I found you upstairs trying to do a faint. Gosh! how you frightened me! Talk about ghosts—I thought I saw one of them."

"But I'm better now. I am getting warmer and better every minute."

"I can't have you fainting in coils all over the floor and making a sensation."

"I didn't quite faint, Percy. Only lost consciousness about half a minute."

"How do you know that? It might have been three-quarters. Now, don't you honestly think you'd better stop at home to-night? We shall be very late, anyhow."

"No, no, let's go. It will do me good. I don't want to sit in this horrid house all the evening."

Cookie appeared at the door, with Nanny behind her, at this moment.

"I hope you're better, 'm," she said anxiously. "What was it made you faint, I wonder?"

She had, of course, her own private opinion, which she had just imparted to Nanny, but that does not concern us here.

"Oh, I don't know, Cookie, I'm sure. Something upset me at dinner, I expect. Perhaps I hurried over it too much. But I'm quite all right now, thank you, and we're just going to the dance."

The maids went away, to talk over the matter in their own domain, and Percy asked:

"Are you really fit, Life of my Life? You don't look a very good colour yet."

"Then I'll put some on," she said impishly, with a grimace at him. "Isn't it queer, Percy, how we love reading ghost stories? I never realized before how horrible it is to see . . . " She broke off with a shudder.

"Don't think of it. If we're going to the dance, let's go at once. I'll fetch the car round."

"No. I'll come with you and get in at the garage."

"Better stay here in the warm. I won't be two minutes."

"If you think I am going to be left two minutes alone here, Mr. Percy Dacre, Esquire, you are very much mistaken," Peggy declared. "I'm coming with you."

"Goose-bird!"

"You'd be a gander if you'd seen what I have," she retorted.

"By Jove!" Percy chuckled, as he put on his overcoat, "the old nursery rhyme comes true!" and he quoted:

"Goosie, goosie, gander,

Whither shall I wonder,
Upstairs, downstairs, in my lady's chamber—
There I met an old man
Who wouldn't say his prayers . . .

"I say, Peg, perhaps that's why he . . . "

"Oh, don't scoff, Perks. I don't feel as if I could stand it to-night."

The yard lay in darkness and Peggy shuddered again, glancing over her shoulder as Percy went into the garage and started the car. They were soon running smoothly along the road to the town and were not so very late at the dance.

They both loved dancing, and, it is unnecessary to say, were good dancers. There was an excellent band and the floor was just right. Peggy felt her spirits rise and was happy in the consciousness that no woman wore a prettier frock than her own or had a handsomer husband. But towards midnight she began to flag. The experience she had gone through that night could not be without effect on a highly strung nervous system, and Percy soon realized that her strength was spent. He insisted upon taking her home before the last dance and she did not offer a very determined resistance.

Her last words to him that night were:

"I shall write to Mr. Marsh in the morning."

CHAPTER XXIII

THE date was fixed, the letter of invitation despatched to Mr. Marsh, and the invitation was promptly accepted. Peggy braced herself to meet the situation and Percy was resigned, though he dreaded the visit of the "long-haired one." But he was worried about his wife who began to show herself decidedly off colour and unlike herself. It was plain enough to him that her nerves were in a lamentable state. She was so "jumpy" that any sudden noise, however slight, made her start and tremble. She never dared to go upstairs alone after dark and slept fitfully, often screaming in her sleep. There were shadows under her eyes, her appetite had fallen off, and she had become strangely irritable; catching at straws of offence and showing a hysterical tendency to tears on slight provocation.

Percy was, as he expressed it, "fed to the back teeth" with all this, and had begun to hunt through papers for advertisements of houses. For he had no faith in the Psychical Society's emissaries and did not expect Mr. Marsh to have any success in his 'spook finding.' Peggy must do as she wished; opposition would only make matters worse; but he saw no clear way out of trouble save another move, at whatever the cost.

It was a nuisance. He didn't want to leave Leatheringham, the friends he had made, the garden he had begun to love. February had opened with exceptional beauty; the skies were clear, the air soft; little blue squills with hepaticas, snowdrops, and crocuses, were beginning to paint the borders, and aconites shone like golden stars in the grass under the trees. Birds sang at dawn, tassels hung from the nut bushes and the branches of tree and bush were reddening with buds. 'Hell Corner' was just becoming an Eden and Percy revelled in the sweet country air and a bigger garden than he had ever possessed before. He was never likely to get another such home at the price he had paid for this, and was well aware of the fact. But if Peggy could not be happy here, they must leave it. No doubt of that existed in his mind. So he hunted through the house agents' advertisements diligently.

Peggy was all right in the daytime. She enjoyed the garden as much as he did; her work in the house and many engagements kept her busy, and Percy took her for a long run in the car every afternoon. But as soon as dusk fell she grew nervy; started and looked over her shoulder at every sound, peered at every shadow, and hated to be left alone a minute.

Percy did not know what to do about having electric light laid on in the house. He had an idea that it might put 'the spook' to flight. But suppose it did not, and the haunting, or whatever it was, persisted? He would have had all the expense for nothing and they would have to go all the same.

He had a shrewd notion, too, that a move would cause suspicions which would greatly militate against his selling the house. Everyone would want to know why they were leaving such a desirable residence. Already the place had not a good name. Its late owner had made himself unpopular, and the name 'Hell Corner' had been given to it. No doubt the story of strange sights and noises had oozed out in the town, although he and Peggy had not been told of it; their friends had too much tact for that. But *talk*, in a country town, spreads a spark of suggestion to a flame with no limits in a very short time, and it was most unlikely that Cook and Nanny had kept the account of Susan Cleaver's sudden fright and the children's "funny old man" to themselves. They, like the Dacres, had made friends in the neighbourhood, and it would be a wonder if they had resisted the temptation of telling so thrilling a story. So if the house were put up for sale again so soon, Percy felt sure, there would be no buyers: or if one, in desperate need of a home, did come forward, he would expect to get it for a mere song. There had not been a great demand for The Beeches before: there would probably be less now.

Had any suggestion of haunting cheapened it from the first? he began to question now, remembering certain floating sentences caught at the sale. No one had told him so, but was it likely they would? Most people are ashamed of even a lurking belief in ghosts, and nobody is inclined to enlighten a stranger as to any defects in a house he is buying. "Mind your own business" is a proverb strictly observed, as a rule, by men, and almost as strictly by women. In this case there had really been no opportunity for enlightenment, and if anybody had attempted it, Percy knew very well that he would have laughed to scorn any such warning. No one in the world could ever have made him believe that, in less than six months, he would be contemplating selling his house because there was a ghost in it!

But he had to face the fact now. The ghost, whether a genuine spiritual phenomenon or strange effect of light and shadow operating on imaginative minds—as he persuaded himself—was upsetting his life and driving him from the house. It would be impossible to go on living in it much longer, if the trouble did not cease.

His uncomfortable suspicion that rumours of the haunting might be filtering through to the neighbours was confirmed on the day of the children's party. Peggy had invited about a dozen youngsters, from three to seven years of age, and with the smallest babies had asked the mothers. They played in the garden till four o'clock; after which an exciting "goblin hunt" followed. Peggy had spent several evenings manufacturing tiny red goblins out of crinkled paper, and these were hidden in the hall and all the downstairs rooms. Every child who found a goblin had it changed for a small gift, and as it grew dusk the fun became more thrilling. It was when the first lamp was being lighted that Percy heard one young mother say to Peggy:

"Don't you find lamp and candle-light very unked?"

Peggy, who had never heard this local word, asked what it meant.

"Oh . . . weird, you know, and ghostly. One could easily fancy things in the shadows."

Not to be drawn, Peggy only laughed and said they were getting used to lamplight now. At first it had certainly seemed queer.

But the lady was not to be put off, and Percy, pretending to hunt for goblins, with a small thing of three clutching his finger, heard her say:

"Some people declare this house is haunted. Isn't it silly, the tales that get about? Of course you've never seen or heard anything?"

"Of course not," said Peggy promptly, and changed the subject.

That was all. But it struck a definite blow at Percy's hope of selling the house. And when her visitors had all gone, he said so to Peggy."

"I heard Mrs. Campion informing you that our house is haunted," he observed, as they sat down to rest after a hectic time; "a straw showing the way of the wind. I expect they're gabbing about it all over the town."

"Let them," retorted Peggy. "It won't hurt us."

"Oh, won't it, madam? Suppose we want to let, or sell the house, who'll take it, if they hear it's full of spooks?"

Peggy reflected a moment. She had not thought of this. Then she said:

"Well, we're not thinking of selling the house, are we?"

Percy did not reply at once. He had said nothing to her about his search through house agents' advertisements.

"Are you prepared to stay on here," he asked, presently, "if old Barker keeps on cropping up and driving you silly?"

"I know you think I'm silly, Perks, but you needn't be so offensive as to say so."

"The truth is often offensive, my Precious Pegtop, but that is neither here nor there. The point is, do you think you will ever get used to the old gentleman, or whatever it is that scares you to fits? It isn't merely a psychological question. It's a mighty material one, since, if we have to scuttle out of the house, we shall probably drop about a thousand pounds on it. I am glad you squashed the silly ass with a thumping fib. But there's no smoke without fire, and I strongly suspect the domestics in this little circle have been jabbering about our spook. What do you think?"

"It looks like it," said Peggy, with a sigh.

They stared gloomily into the fire for some minutes, and then she brightened.

"Let's hope Mr. Marsh can find out something," she exclaimed. "I've great faith in him."

"What on earth you think he can do beats me," said Percy, sceptically.

"He might get into touch with——" she paused.

"And he might not. What then?"

"We must hope for the best. Some people say spirits can only haunt the place of their former life for a short time after death. I read that somewhere."

"And I've read somewhere that old houses are haunted for centuries," he replied, grimly. "Have you never heard of Glamis Castle? There's a persistent ghost for you—and a malignant one at that!"

"Of course that's true," said Peggy, sadly. "But perhaps we can find the missing will."

"Oh, you still believe in that missing will? Bless the innocent child! A long course of detective melodrama has moulded her plastic mind."

"There must be some reason, Percy."

"Agreed. Well, let it be a missing will, if you like. But if there is, why on earth doesn't the old fool let us know where it is hidden, after the accepted traditional manner? He has only to stand still, point, and gibber!"

"When he did appear I was too terrified to look at him. Perhaps he has been trying to point out the spot."

"Well, I only wish he'd appear to me," said Percy, complacently. "He would find me ready to carry out his instructions."

"I wonder! You sceptics are very easily scared," Peggy observed.

"I suppose you think the long-haired spook-finder won't be so easily scared. For your sake I hope he won't. And I promise you this, my Queen of Hearts, if he manages this job well, finds the missing will and lays the ghost, I'll subscribe to his Society and admit that there are 'more things in heaven and earth than are dreamed of' in my capacity. If Shakespeare believed in ghosts, why shouldn't your humble Perks?"

"Why not, indeed," said Peggy.

But the "long-haired spook-finder" did not lay the ghost; did not even come to Hell Corner. And the reason for this will be related in the next chapter.

CHAPTER XXIV

THAT night the devoted parents, who had romped for about three hours with their own and other folks' children, slept soundly. But at the darkest hour in the night, when Percy was in the middle of a pleasant dream, beating Bogie on the golf course, he felt his arm suddenly clutched and heard a voice close to his ear say, in a low tone, full of blood-curdling terror:

"Perks! Perks! Listen!"

Only half-awake and feeling sure that Peggy's nerves were solely responsible for this annoying intrusion into his dream, Percy growled: "Oh, chuck it, Peg, and go to sleep. Don't bother me."

"There's something moving in the room downstairs, Percy. You *must* hear it," she said, giving his arm another little shake. "Don't go to sleep again, for goodness' sake."

Next moment he was sitting up in bed wide-awake. For there was a distinct sound in the drawing-room below, as of heavy furniture being moved about.

"By gosh! Does the fool think he can make a noise like that without disturbing the whole house!" he exclaimed irritably, and sprang out of bed.

"What are you going to do?" Peggy gasped.

"Going to see what he's up to. Where's my electric torch? Oh, here it is."

He thrust his feet into bedroom slippers and opened the door very softly.

"Oh, don't leave me, Perks!" cried Peggy, in terror.

The noise went slowly on.

"Don't be silly. Put your head under the clothes," he said, ruthlessly. And then, arming himself with one of the heavy dumb-bells he used for morning exercises, Percy crept quietly downstairs.

Peggy did not put her head under the bed-clothes. She was not quite such an arrant coward as that. If Percy went to face danger, she must go too. Springing out of bed, she flung on a wrapper and stood listening at her door. There was a night-light burning in the room—she couldn't sleep without one now.

Crash!!

Her heart stood still a moment. Then, snatching up the other dumb-bell, she fled downstairs.

The drawing-room was in total darkness, when Peggy reached the threshold, but the next moment a ray from Percy's torch was flashed upon the door and round to the window. She could see him, very dimly, picking himself up from the floor, but there was no sight nor sound of any other being. He was swearing softly to himself.

"Perks! Are you all right? What was it?" she gasped. He did not answer immediately, and the light travelled everywhere about the room. She saw, then, that there had been a smash. The fire-screen was lying on the floor with its glass in fragments all over the carpet. Percy rubbing one elbow in the shadow, came towards her.

"What was it?" she asked again.

"Dashed if I know. Nothing, apparently. What a bally fool I am! I've smashed your old fire-screen up to smithereens."

She drew a long breath of relief and grabbed his arm, for she felt tottery.

"What does it matter about the old screen so long as you are all right? But you gave me an awful fright, Perks. I expected to find you in a pool of gore. Tell me what happened."

"I fell over the bally thing. I could have sworn I saw it moving, and, of course, I thought some one was behind it. Naturally I went for it and hit out with the dumb-bell. There was nothing!"

"Well?"

"I lost my balance and came an awful cropper. Look out for the glass; it's all over the place. Silly ass, that I am, walking in my sleep. For, of course, I was only half-awake."

"Percy, what nonsense! You were wide-awake."

"Couldn't have been, my Own. No man in his senses could fancy he saw furniture moving when there was no one else near. I couldn't be quite such a fool as that if I hadn't been half-asleep."

"Are you so sure the screen didn't move?"

"Of course I'm sure. How could it? No, I was dreaming, obviously. Come on back to bed, my child, and don't stand shivering there with such saucer eyes. Why did you come down? I told you to put your head under the clothes."

"As if I should when you might be in danger!"

Glancing down he saw, for the first time, the dumb-bell in her hand.

"Brave little Angel! Did she expect to brain the ghost, then? It's a mercy she didn't do her own Perks in by mistake. And no shoes on her pretty feet either! Do be careful where you tread."

"I didn't stop to think. I saw you snatch a dumb-bell, so I did the same."

"Imitation is the sincerest form of valour."

He took the dumb-bell from her, giving her the torch in exchange, and then, taking her in his arms, he carried her up to their room, professing to puff and pant when he got inside and declaring that she must have put on a lot of weight since he last did so.

There she had to stay alone, for a few minutes, while he went over the house, flashing his lamp into every corner. She wanted to go with him, but Percy would not have her.

"If I meet the ruffian, I'll yell for help," he promised, "and you can come along with the dumb-bell. But I shan't find anybody. It's a mere matter of form. When there's a noise in your house, you are supposed to go round it and try all the doors and windows."

He was soon back.

"I found him in the larder, eating tarts," he said. "I told him the Queen of Hearts would be after him, but he only laughed. So then I kicked him out, the knave! What would you have done?"

"Made him pay for the broken glass."

"I never thought of that," said Percy.

They laughed, like children, over this make-believe.

When they were in bed again, Peggy said: "Seriously, Perks, aren't you satisfied now?"

"Satisfied! You mean satiated?"

"No, I mean, can you doubt any longer that there is something strange in this house, some supernatural agency at work which cannot be accounted for in any ordinary way? You heard the noise plainly. You said so. You went downstairs expecting to find a man there, and you found nothing. Confess now, Percy, that there must have been *something*. It would be a violation of the laws governing cause and effect if those sounds we both heard were caused by—*nothing*. You won't own it, because you think I shall be only more frightened. But I can't be that. You have admitted that you saw the screen move. What moved it?"

After a pause he said: "I thought I saw it move, certainly, but the light may have deceived me—or my sleepy state. There is such a thing as an optical illusion, Peg."

"Yes, and there's such a thing as an obstinate sceptic, Perks.

If you hadn't heard a noise you wouldn't have gone down. What made it?"

"I suppose you think it was made by a—what do you call it?—a 'discarnate intelligence.' But for the life of me, I can't conceive how a 'discarnate intelligence' can shove heavy furniture about."

"I suppose they have a peculiar force that we know nothing of. Perhaps they can permeate matter. I've seen a table move, dance on one leg, and shoot across a room with no one touching it."

"Oh, come now, Pegtop—'with no one *touching* it'! 'And has my darling told a lie'?"

"Your darling has not. I've seen the table move so suddenly and swiftly that no hands could keep on it. After all, Percy, what do we know about the forces underlying matter? It would be no more wonderful for spirit to move furniture than it is for electric current to drive an engine. You can't *see* the current. You don't even know what it is. You only know what it can do. You don't know what a ghost can do, and you assume it can't do anything."

Percy made no reply. His scepticism had certainly received a shock, but he was very reluctant to admit this. There is nothing we hate more than giving up our disbeliefs. All his life Percy had disbelieved in ghosts and he wanted to continue in that happy state of scepticism. But he was by nature frank, and so he said at last:

"Well, I'll own I'm baffled. Is that enough for you, Star of my Soul? Or must I declare that I believe this blessed house is haunted?"

"You may as well say so, Perks, for you must believe it, after to-night."

"Very well, then. Consider it said, my Poppet, and let us sleep in peace. My! Won't Cookie have a fit when she sees that mess in the drawing-room to-morrow morning?"

A fresh view of the affair was raised; a fresh problem. What were they to tell the maids? For some time they cogitated over this, trying to find the most likely, most plausible and least mendacious lie they could think of. Percy hit on it eventually and they went to sleep satisfied.

CHAPTER XXV

COOKIE was indeed inexpressibly shocked at the sight that met her eyes when she went to draw the curtains and open the windows of the drawing-room. She called Nanny and, together, they gaped at the wrecked pole-screen, whose head had come off its stand and whose glass was scattered all over the carpet.

"Whatever on earth could they have been up to last night?" ejaculated Cookie, "I thought I heard something, didn't you, Rose?"

"Yes, but I've heard so many funny noises in this house at night I never take no notice of them now," said Nanny. "Do you s'pose it was Mr. and Mrs. Dacre having a dance together, or something of that sort? You never now what they'll do. They're like children themselves—so full of fun and all that."

"Not likely," her friend observed. "There's other things disturbed—look at that sofa. It seems to me as somebody's got into the house and we ought to send for the police at once. If it was burglars there's no time to lose in gitting on their track."

To this Nanny agreed, and Cookie ran upstairs to knock at her employer's door, nearly an hour before the usual time.

"Hullo!" cried Percy. "What is it?"

"If you please, sir, I thought you ought to know——"

"Come in," he said, before she got any further, for her voice was muffled. Cookie put her head into the room.

"I thought you ought to know at once, sir, as some one's been into the house in the night," she said. "The droring-room is in a horful state, with the fire-screen smashed and glass all over the shop. Would you like me to send Judkins to the police-station?"

"Er . . . no, thank you, Cookie. It's all right. We know all about it," Percy responded cheerfully: "In fact—er—we did it—at least, I did. I was just showing Mrs. Dacre a few exercises with the dumb-bells and—er—my foot slipped. I fell over the screen and smashed it."

He was not a very expert liar and it struck him, in this unveracious narrative, that it was a little thin in parts. Why, for instance, should he bring the dumb-bells down to the drawing-room to show Mrs. Dacre his exercises, when he did them every morning in his room? But, fortunately for him, the average mind does not reason and is ready to accept what it is told without question. Cookie went back to the kitchen.

"Just like a schoolboy," she said to Nanny. "Fancy doing dumb-bell exercises in the droring-room like that! What next, I wonder? You might come and help me pick up the bits of glass, Rose, or it'll take me half the morning.

After breakfast, Percy, who fancied himself as an amateur carpenter, thought he could mend the screen. But he soon saw that the job was beyond him; or, at any rate, beyond his tools. So he took it, in the car, down to the principal furniture dealer in the town, a man of some standing, and a fellow-golfer, named Ballam.

"How did you manage to smash it up like this?" he asked. "It looks as if you'd been dancing on it!"

Percy could think of no better story than the one he had invented for Cookie.

"I was giving my wife an exhibition of skill with the dumb-bells," he said, laughing, "and my foot slipped. I went right over on it."

"I hope you didn't cut yourself with the glass."

"No, luckily I didn't. It's a wonder. Do you think you can put it right for me? The work doesn't seem to be injured, though the wood of the stand is splintered."

Mr. Ballam assured him, after examining the screen, that there was no harm done that could not quite easily be mended. He admired the beauty of the antique and told Percy he should have it back within the week.

Just after tea that day, at the "children's hour," when Gib, K., Fliss, and Billikin were pretending to be ravening wolves come to gobble Daddy and Mummie up, and making the noise of twenty wolves, Cookie came into the room and tried to make herself heard above the racket. Percy commanded silence and was then told that Mr. Ballam would like to see Mr. Dacre for a few minutes. The wolves raised a howl of disappointment, baulked of their prey, as Daddy went out; but they were soon after Mummie again.

In the drawing-room the lamp, which Cookie had just lighted, shed its yellow rays on an excited face, as Mr. Ballam came forward.

"I must apologize for calling at this hour, Mr. Dacre," he said, "but I couldn't wait till the morning to tell you something, and you're not on the 'phone, I believe. Your screen, that you brought me this morning——" He paused.

"Well?" Percy caught his excitement and began to anticipate.

"You knew it was valuable, but not *how* valuable to some one, if not yourself. I've found something inside it—between the two pieces of work."

"I know!" exclaimed Percy, with a flash of revelation, "the will."

In thinking the matter over afterwards, he could not imagine why he jumped to that conclusion so promptly. Was it not a complete recantation of all his doubts? Part of the night and nearly all day he had been pondering over the strange thing that had happened, but had not, till this moment, consciously connected it with the suggested missing will, in which he had never really believed. The thought flashed upon him as if by telephone or wireless, from—whence? The subconscious self?

"Yes," said Ballam. "It seems to be—it *is*, in fact—a will made by the late Benjamin Barker, who formerly lived here, as you know . . . May I ask if you became possessed of the screen at his sale?"

"I did. My wife fell in love with it, so I bought it. Whereabouts was it? You said, I think, between the panels of needlework."

"Yes, and the wonder of it is, I very nearly missed it. I was feeling round the edges, with no idea of finding anything of course, and I felt there was a space filled up with paper. It was the curious texture of the paper that struck me. I probed further and found it was parchment. When I drew it out and saw the name, Benjamin Barker, it gave me quite a turn. There has been a lot of talk, you know, about the old gentleman dying intestate, after promising legacies to several people, and telling them he had made a will. It seemed so extraordinary for me to find it—quite accidentally, like that, and by the merest chance. Why on earth did he hide it there?"

"Goodness only knows! He was an eccentric character, I believe."

"Eccentric to the verge of . . . but a clever businessman all the same. There was a strange kink in him. It is difficult to believe that any sane man could make a will and then hide it where no one was ever likely to find it. And tell nobody! That is the marvel."

"What have you done with it?" asked Percy.

"Brought it to you. I didn't know what to do with it, and as the screen was yours I thought you had a right to its contents. Here it is!"

He fished the very legal-looking document out of his overcoat pocket and handed it to Percy, adding: "I suppose you will write at once to the lawyers who are named here, a London firm. Strange they should not have heard of their client's death. The announcement of it was sent to *The Times* and other papers."

"Strange indeed," Percy assented as he took the document. Privately, he was thinking: "Not half so strange as other things I could mention," and he felt a slight squirm of the nerves as he recalled the thing he had seen the night before—that pole-screen moving across the carpet towards him, unimpelled by any living force. Aloud he said:

"I am very much obliged to you, Mr. Ballam, for bringing this up to me at once. Of course the will is no affair of mine, but if it is a question of justice being done, the sooner it is made known the better. Perhaps the best plan will be for me to go to town and find these lawyers to-morrow. Unless you think I ought to hand the document to anyone else?"

"I don't think so. He had quarrelled with all the lawyers here. But it is for you to decide."

The door opened and Peggy entered, closing it behind her to shut out the noise of the children. She stood waiting a moment, with expectant eyes.

"Well?" she said, interrogatively.

"My wife, Mr. Ballam."

Peggy, recalled to good manners, greeted him politely. Then she asked quickly:

"Haven't you found something inside the screen, Mr. Ballam?"

"I have," he answered, looking rather surprised, "I've just handed it to Mr. Dacre. Did you suspect there was something hidden there?"

"I knew there was," said Peggy. "I felt certain of it as soon as I heard you had called."

Then she turned to Percy: "Now aren't you convinced?"

Seeing the puzzled look on Ballam's face, Percy observed, blandly: "My wife has always felt convinced that there was a will and suspected it to be somewhere in the house."

"I am glad to tell you you were right, Mrs. Dacre," said Ballam. "I shall not, of course, mention this affair to anyone until after the will is proved; and I know you will not. Now, I must wish you good night."

When he had gone, they returned to the morning-room, where the 'wolves,' so long deprived of their prey, fastened on them again for their last few minutes before bedtime. There was no chance of discussion until the children had been carried off by Nanny.

Whereupon Peggy asked: "Have you looked at it, Perks?"

"Not yet. We will read it together now."

"Yes, and then I will go and tell Susan Cleaver."

"You mustn't do that, Peg, till we've communicated with the lawyers. Didn't you hear what Ballam said? He was quite right. The will must be proved before the matter is mentioned to a soul. I shall take it to the London lawyers to-morrow."

"Wouldn't writing do?"

"No—better see them. The fact that they've never communicated with anyone here looks as if something had happened. There may have been a death in the firm, or a dissolution of partnership—or change of address. I must look them up."

"What harm could there be in my telling Susan the will is found?"

"There might be harm. In the first place it might raise her hopes only to be disappointed. He may not have left her anything?"

"Well, aren't we going to look?"

"There might be some legal defect in the will, even if he did leave her a legacy."

"Not likely. Why should there? Anyhow, let's see it."

They studied the will together.

"It seems all right," said Percy, when they had struggled through the legal jungle of unpunctuated sentences, in archaic language, with more or less understanding: "Apparently he has left Susan Nipper—I mean Susan Cleaver, quite a tidy income.[16] I don't think there can be any mistake, but one never knows with lawyers—what they'll find to dispute."

"I'm sure it's plain enough. Do let me go and tell her, Perks, it would give her such a gloriously happy night."

"To-morrow will do, I think, Peg. After waiting about a year, she can wait twenty-four hours longer. We'd better sleep on it, I think. You can go and tell her while I'm in London. You can drive me to the station and call on your way back."

This recalled something to Peggy. She gave a start.

"Why, Perks, we've forgotten. Mr. Marsh is arriving to-morrow at 3.15. We must wire him at once. Or is it too late now?" She looked at her wrist-watch.

"What are you going to wire for?" asked Percy. "It doesn't matter if I'm not here. We might come down by the same train."

She stared at him.

"But we don't want him now," she said. "There's no need for him to come."

"Why not?"

"Percy, surely you realize that we shan't be troubled any more now that the will is found."

"How do you know that?"

"Because there will be no reason for it. Do be honest, darling,

[16] Susan Nipper is a character from *Dombey and Son* by Charles Dickens.

and admit that there *was* a reason for all we have seen and heard. Doesn't this prove it? Don't pretend any more. Don't stick it out that the noise we both heard last night was imaginary. You *know* it wasn't. Be rational, Perks, and don't set a mere prejudice against the law of cause and effect. It was *you* who saw the thing move; *you* through whom the will has been found. You can't get away from that. Don't be mulish and unreasonable, Percy."

He looked into her earnest eyes and the smile died on his lips.

"All right, Sweet, I recant. I'll believe in just this one ghost, to oblige you. But on one condition only—that it effaces itself and never worries us again. Will that do?"

"He will never worry us again," said Peggy, with conviction. "You'll see."

And she was right.

It was too late to send a telegram to Mr. Marsh that night, but Peggy wrote him an explanatory letter, and the wire was sent in good time next morning.

CHAPTER XXVI

PEGGY did not find it easy to write her letter to Mr. Marsh and request him not to come, after inviting him. The mere statement, unbalanced by any argument save her own conviction, that the haunting of her house was unlikely to persist, seemed, as Percy said, "a trifle thin." After tearing up many sheets of her best note-paper, she finally wrote:

"DEAR MR. MARSH,

"I am glad to tell you that something has occurred in our house which, I believe, will make any further investigation unnecessary. Last night we heard strange sounds below and my husband went down, prepared to encounter a burglar. In going for the man, as he thought, he fell over, and smashed, an old pole-screen, which disclosed a will made by the former owner of the house, whose spirit, I have long believed, has haunted us. My husband is seeing the lawyers to-day, and if he finds all is in order, and the will is proved, I have not the slightest doubt that we shall be no more troubled in this matter. If I should be wrong in this surmise, I will write to you again and request your aid. Thanking you for your kind offer to come and investigate, I am, yours truly,

"MARGARET DACRE."

She posted her letter on the way to the station, where she drove Percy, and on her return called at the small house, in a mean street where Susan Cleaver had taken up her abode, in two rooms.

The door was opened almost before the car stopped, somewhat to Peggy's surprise. She was more surprised when Susan explained.

"Come in, ma'am. I have been expecting you."

"Why was that?" Peggy asked, as she followed Susan into her small bed-sitting-room, where a scanty fire burned in the grate, and a pile of linen on the table showed that the poor woman was trying to eke out her savings with plain sewing. The bed was hidden behind a screen.

"I knew you were coming this morning," she said, and, looking at her, Peggy noted a pink spot on each cheek-bone and a strange light in her eyes.

"You knew!" exclaimed Peggy. "How could you know?"

"I dreamt of you last night," was the reply, as Peggy sat down by the fire, drawing Susan down to the chair beside her. "I dreamt you stood by my bed and said: "Don't cry, Susan, you needn't cry any more. I'm coming to tell you good news to-morrow.' Then I woke, and my pillow was wet with tears. Not that *that* was anything new. I am quite tired sometimes of a morning with crying in my sleep. But this time, I didn't feel unhappy and I went to sleep and didn't dream any more. When I woke this morning, I felt a sort of lightness of heart, and I knew you were coming. Is there any . . . has anything happened, ma'am?"

"Yes, there has." Peggy grasped both her hands and shook them. "Something wonderful has happened, Susan"—the name came naturally to her lips—"and I've come to congratulate you. *The will is found.*"

With a low cry Susan drew away her hands, covered her face, and sobbed unrestrainedly. Peggy let her weep. She knew the relief it must be after all these months of despair, of hope deferred, and heart-sickness.

She knew, also, that the woman's wretchedness had not been caused by the lack of an expected legacy so much as by the cruel disappointment of feeling that her devotion had been unrecognized and that the one human creature to whom she had given her affection, had betrayed her to penury in her old age—as her next stammering words conclusively showed.

"You'll think, ma'am," she sobbed, when she could speak at all, "that I'm a mercenary woman . . . as thinks of nothing but money. But it's not that . . . it's . . . I thought as how he had forgotten me, and what he promised . . . and what people thought and said about him . . . it all cut me to the quick . . . to say what they did about him being mean and false, and getting work out of us cheap by telling us we was to be recompensated when he died. I knew he was a good man, though odd in his ways, and really meant well; only people didn't pay such good wages in his young days and he hated change and all that. Oh, I am so thankful—so very thankful the will is found, to put a stop to all the lies about him. Have you read it, ma'am?"

Peggy said that she had and that her husband had gone to London to find the lawyers. She then told Susan all that had occurred two nights ago, enjoying the narrative and thrill of it, which she was easily able to communicate to the listener by her side. Susan sat with clasped hands and wide eyes, drinking in the story, with little gasps and exclamations at intervals. When Peggy came to the part where Percy fell over, and smashed, the screen, she gave a little shriek.

"I might have known! I might have known!" she cried. "He always said I was to have the screen, and how valuable it was. To think I never thought of it all that time I was alone in the house and could have taken it to pieces without anyone knowing! To think of it! Of course it was in the screen, Mrs. Dacre!"

"Yes, it was. It was too badly broken for us to mend, so my

husband took it, next morning, to Mr. Ballam and left it there. Last evening, when we were having our usual game with the children after tea, he came up and asked to see Mr. Dacre. As soon as I heard his name I felt sure the will had been found. It came over me just as you said it did over you in your dream, and when Percy didn't come back I went into the room and said so. They were surprised that I knew without being told."

Susan interrupted: "You were told ma'am; *he* told you."

"Very likely. Anyhow, I felt sure enough. Mr. Ballam told us he found the parchment between two pieces of work. You may remember, that they were not quite the same both sides, as is most usual with those old fire-screens; there being a picture of a girl and a young man one side, and a flower design on the other. Well, between the two there was this double sheet of parchment, and it was only by the merest accident that he found it. If he hadn't, Susan, my dear woman, the screen would have been mended with it closed up again as before, and, perhaps, never found at all."

"It would," asserted Susan, solemnly. "He would have given you no peace till it was. I'm as certain of that as that I'm sitting here."

Peggy was not disposed to deny this. She only said: "Well, thank goodness the will is found, anyhow. But what on earth could have induced a sane man to hide his will where it might possibly never be found beats me! It's incredible that anyone could be so idiotic."

"Susan Cleaver looked at her with eyes that seemed to pierce through her body to something behind her. She was silent a few moments. Then she said:

"He meant me to find it. It's me that is to blame, not him. I've been a fool—a blind fool. He told me I was to have the screen and impressed its value upon me, over and over again, yet I never understood, and when the gentleman came to take an inventory of his things I didn't like to say he'd given it to me. I was afraid they wouldn't believe me and think I was trying to pinch what wasn't mine. I'd die rather than anyone should think that."

"But it was extraordinarily silly of him not to tell you the will was in it. He must have been mad!" exclaimed Peggy.

"He was a little mad, on some points. I've often thought so. But you mustn't forget ma'am, that he was took very sudden at the last. He never expected to die like that, without any warning, being a fine healthy man for his years. Once or twice, the week before, he complained of a little dizziness in the head, but it did not worry me, or him, because he'd had it before and nothing came of it. Then the stroke came and he couldn't speak again. No doubt he meant to tell me but——"

She broke off suddenly and her eyes dilated. Peggy waited for her to go on, but she didn't.

"What are you thinking of?" she asked, at last. Susan took a deep breath before replying.

"I never though of it till now," she said, "but I remember now, as he lay helpless before the doctor came . . . I had to run out and catch some one passing to fetch the doctor, for I daren't leave him . . . well, when I got back to Mr. Barker, he had recovered a little consciousness, and tried hard to speak to me. He kept saying, over and over again, 'the sea, the sea'—or so it sounded to me. I wondered what he could mean. And when the doctor came and we got him to bed, he kept making the same sort of hissing sound and another that was like 'key'—sometimes it was like 'shee.' I've often thought of it since and wondered what he was trying to say. I thought, at the time, it might be 'key' and that he wanted to tell me about something he had locked up. Of course I never connected it with his will. I expected that was with the lawyers all right. But now I understand what he was struggling to say. It was 'the screen,' and he could not speak the word properly. Oh, why didn't I think of it before?"

Tears sprang into her eyes again, as she went on.

"He must have put it there on that evening when he sent me out for a walk. I remember it because it was so unusual for him to tell me to go out. He never seemed to think I needed fresh air and exercise, or any change. But that night he said I looked pale and a walk would do me good. When I got back he said he had been carpentering. Oh! how well I remember it all now! He had some tools and used to love messing about with them, making seed boxes and putting up shelves in his store-room—that little room Mr. Dacre uses now. I expect that was when he took the screen to pieces and put the will inside it. I smelt glue, but I never saw anything he'd made that night. He seemed very pleased with himself over something, and was smiling and rubbing his hands, like he always used to do when he was pleased. I often think of that smile of his, ma'am. It was such a queer smile—a silly smile I used to think. Yet he wasn't silly in most ways."

"I should think one way was enough!" ejaculated Peggy. "He really must have been mad, Susan. You can't convince me that any sane man would take all that trouble to hide his will. Why should he?"

"I can't say, ma'am. Except that he was so suspicious of everyone, especially lawyers. I've often heard him say as he wouldn't trust a lawyer on his Bible oath. Yet I suppose—you said—that he had a lawyer from London to make his will."

"He certainly did."

"Well, I know he wouldn't trust anyone here. He thought everybody in Leatheringham was against him. There was that queer twist in his mind. He didn't like anybody much—except children. He was always fond of children and gave a lot of money to orphanages. He was good to old people too. But he hated all his neighbours and loved to annoy them. He thought they hated him and wanted to injure him. I had to keep all the doors locked and bolted, and he kept the dogs chained up to make them savage, for the same reason. He was funny in some ways."

Peggy could not control a little peal of laughter.

"He must have been funny to the verge of lunacy!" she exclaimed; "and if I were you, Susan, I wouldn't tell all this to other people, or you may lose your legacy. I hear the late Mr. Barker's cousin is a very greedy and unscrupulous man. He may dispute the will on the ground that his cousin was of unsound mind when he made it."

Susan's face changed, but only for a moment. She smiled.

"He couldn't very well prove that, ma'am, seeing as Mr. Barker—*my* Mr. Barker—was at business up to the day he died, and kept all his books perfect—and all that. But if he did—if he claimed every penny of the money, and got it, I shouldn't mind now. I need the money, of course, and should be very thankful to feel I was independent, and needn't work hard all the rest of my life. But whether I get it or not, Mr. Barker's character will be cleared of any wrong to me—or Judkins, or the old men at the works, what served him all their lives and were promised a bit. And that is more to me than money, Mrs. Dacre, you'll believe that. To know as he *did* think of me, is enough. I can die happy. For I don't mind telling you, who have been so kind to me—and I know it won't go any further—as I loved that gentleman dearly. I would have done anything in the world for him, and when he died the world went black for me."

Peggy felt her throat swell. She was a good lover herself and could appreciate this passionate affection in another woman.

"Her romance," she reflected. "He was old and plain and a bit mad, a real old curmudgeon, but she loved him. Aren't women queer? They must love some one—a man for choice! Poor Susan, poor old unhappy ghost! He may have loved her too, though he 'always treated her respectful.' Thank goodness he'll trouble us no more."

Aloud she said:

"He couldn't have been such a bad sort, or he wouldn't have won the affection of a good woman like yourself. And he must have cared a lot for you, to have haunted this earth when he might have entered into a happier one. I believe all you say. I know you care more about his reputation than you do about his money. Now I must go"—impulsively she bent and kissed her. "I congratulate you on this happy ending, and I feel sure everything will be all right. Come up and hear what my husband has to say this evening."

Susan struggled with her tears and tried to utter words of gratitude, but in vain. She could only wring Peggy's little hand in her own large, work-hardened one, and say nothing.

CHAPTER XXVII

THE next few hours dragged with Peggy, as hours will when one is bottling up excitement and impatience. At last she could keep her inward turmoil to herself no longer, but felt impelled to unload it on Cookie, as she was laying the table for lunch.

"I think I must tell you why Mr. Dacre has gone to London, Cookie," she said; "Mr. Barker's will has come to light. It was drawn up by London lawyers, and he has taken it to them. Mr. Ballam found it in the fire-screen."

"Well, I never!" exclaimed Cookie. Her next speech gave Peggy a start.

"So now, I suppose, the Old Man won't trouble us any more," she said.

"What old man?" Peggy asked, evasively.

"Him as the children is always talking about, and what Miss Cleaver saw on Christmas night," was the prompt reply.

"Oh, but that . . . that was all fancy," said Peggy, in some confusion. "It doesn't do to believe what children say; they have such strong imaginations. You and Nanny have never seen anything, have you?"

"No, 'm, but we've heard things at night. Me and Nanny have often talked it over in the morning and wondered if there was anything in what they say."

"Who say? What do they say?"

"Oh, it's common talk, 'm, as old Barker walks. Haven't you heard it?"

Peggy remembered the remarks of her visitor at the children's party and was silent.

"The house has had a bad name ever since he died," pursued Cookie. "Mrs. Judkins told me as nobody round here would buy it. They used to call it 'Hell Corner,' even when he was alive, and that isn't a very nice name to give a house. Me and Nanny didn't like it at all when we first heard it, but we got used to it after a while and didn't mind."

Peggy felt suddenly as if she had been sitting on a powder mine all these months. Suppose the gossip had scared her two valuable "stipendiary aids" and they had given her notice. She drew a long breath.

"I'm very glad you didn't take any notice of such foolish nonsense." she said. "The name was given to the house because of those barking dogs that gave the neighbours no peace night or day. It had nothing to do with . . . with ghosts."

"No, 'm—that's right enough. But still——" Cookie hesitated. "There *was* something funny about this place, wasn't there?"

Peggy was glad she put it in the past tense.

"I've sometimes thought so," she said guardedly.

Cookie was going out of the room when she stopped suddenly, turned round, and asked:

"Don't you believe in ghosts, 'm?"

Thus attacked, Peggy had to come to a swift decision. After a moment's pause, she decided that further prevarication would be bad policy.

"I can't truthfully say I don't, Cookie," she responded; "for I have certainly been unable to account for things I've heard . . . and seen. But if it is true that Mr. Barker's spirit has haunted this house, it has been for a purpose, and that purpose exists no longer.

He had hidden the will, meaning to disclose its hiding-place to Susan Cleaver, and he was suddenly cut off from life without being able to speak. Now that the will is found, there is no necessity for his manifestation. At least, that is how I take it."

Cookie agreed, and then Peggy told her all that Susan Cleaver had said, pledging her to secrecy. It seemed rather cruel, as she knew the girl would dearly love to go and tell all her friends this wonderful story. But it may be doubted whether Cookie kept her pledge!

Peggy was glad that it was her afternoon to have the children, being Nanny's day out. They kept her well amused all the afternoon and helped her to curb her impatience for Percy's news. It was a lovely spring-like day, and they played in the garden till nearly tea-time, making themselves delightfully grubby with small rakes and spades and trowels, planting out double pink daisies, setting seeds, and weeding. In this laudable pursuit Billikin pulled up several bulbs and choice plants, before he was settled in his pram with a collection of toys to console him for the lack of Mother Earth, already well represented on his small person. Fliss squatted by a sand heap making pies with a small flower-pot for an hour or more. When she liked doing a thing she never tired of it, but would go steadily on repeating the action hundreds of times, intensely absorbed and happy. It took some time to get them all clean for tea, but Peggy felt she had spent a healthy and laudable afternoon, far more profitable to body and soul than dozing with a book by the fire.

She met Percy by the 6.15 train, and, after teasing her a little by pretending he had not been able to find the lawyers, he contradicted himself and told her the truth, which was that he had unearthed them and seen their copy of the will, which was quite in order.

They had seen or heard nothing of Benjamin Barker's death, which was not very surprising, Percy thought, after seeing the sole surviving member of the firm, a somewhat doddering old person, in an obviously decayed business that had, probably, never been very flourishing. What had made old Barker put his business in their hands, Percy was unable to discover. He could only surmise that the late partner in the firm, who had died but a year or so before, had been the ruling spirit and had come into touch with Mr. Barker through their common interest in Freemasonry, their possible meeting at some Lodge, or on some Masonic Committee. Since his death his partner had shifted camp, taking offices in a cheaper part of London, and Percy had some difficulty in finding out the new address.

The will provided for large legacies to several charities, chiefly orphanages and children's hospitals in connection with Freemasonry and the trade in which he had been concerned. To his foreman and those men who had served him for many years, sums varying from £1000 to £500. To his gardener, Judkins, a younger man who had only been with him a few years, he left £100, and to Susan Cleaver he left £4000. When all these legacies were paid the residue was to go to his cousin; but it was obviously meant that there should not be any residue to speak of. There had been neither affection nor respect between them. The executors of the will were two prominent Masons in the district (not in Leatheringham—old Barker had washed his hands of his native town!) and Percy foresaw a lively time for them when Daniel Barker discovered his loss!

Susan Cleaver came up before they had finished dinner, and sat talking to the maids in the kitchen without the shadow of doubt in her mind that all was well for her. Indeed, if she had felt any doubt Cookie would have dispelled it. She told Susan that Mr. and Mrs. Dacre were in high spirits, "chaffing and laughing," as they certainly would not have been had there been bad news.

And when Percy, trying to look grave and dignified, told her that, so far as he could tell, there was no reason to question the validity of the will, Susan only said: "Thank you very much indeed, sir, for all you've done and the trouble you've taken. I knew it would be all right. Mr. Barker was a business man, if he *was* queer in some ways, and he wouldn't do a thing like that without seeing as he wasn't cheated. I knew he'd made a will and made it proper, for he told me so, rubbing his hands, like he used, and very pleased with himself. If only he'd told me where he put it! But he loved having little secrets to himself and I've no doubt he chuckled over this one many a time and said to himself—'Susan little thinks the will is in the fire-screen.' That's the sort of thing would have amused him, sir. He was a funny gentleman."

"He was—excessively funny," muttered Percy. "But it hasn't been very funny for you, has it, my good soul?"

"Or for us," murmured Peggy.

"It has been a very narrow squeak that you ever heard any more of the will, I can tell you," Percy went on. "That old lawyer is tottering to his grave, and he wasn't worrying about the will, or Benjamin Barker. I shouldn't wonder if he had forgotten all about it. And if Ballam hadn't happened to see a bit of parchment sticking out, you'd never have heard of it till you met the old boy in a better world."

As before, Susan smiled, with shining eyes of faith.

"I think he would never have rested till I *did* know, sir," she said. "But I'm none the less grateful to you and Mrs. Dacre for all you've done—I shall never forget your kindness—never. It has been more to me than I can say."

She turned away to hide her tears. They promised to let her know when the will was proved, and she went away a tearfully happy woman.

"Well, that's that," said Percy, lighting his pipe. "Now let's forget the pair of 'em and talk about the children."

CHAPTER XXVIII

THE will was proved. Old Job Barker raged and swore he would dispute it on the charge that his cousin was of unsound mind, and under alien influence;[17] but the executors, who both knew Benjamin Barker quite well, declared him to be remarkably shrewd and clear-headed in all matters of business, and that his faculties, before he died, had shown no signs of decay. He was extremely odd, of course; no one attempted to deny that; very cunning and secretive and suspicious; but he knew quite well what he was about, and his sanity in all practical affairs of his life had never been called in question.

As to the accusation of undue influence, of course that was absurd, as not even his housekeeper, who had lived with him so many years, knew about the will, who had drawn it up or where it had been hidden. Moreover, the woman herself, and the men at the works were well-known to be above suspicion.

The executors had never been asked if they would accept the appointment and knew nothing whatever about the will, which had been witnessed by clerks in the lawyer's office. They were, however, delighted to learn that it had been found, and especially pleased by the bequests to the different charities in which they were interested.

For some time Percy continued to glance through the advertisements of house-agents, thinking it as well to be prepared for any more excursions and alarms on the part of, what he called, "Peggy's spook"; or of any fresh developments of her nervous

---

[17] A reference to Job in the Bible, whose fortune was taken from him by Satan.

imagination. For he well knew that fancy is hard to kill, and whether the apparition were of fancy or not, he might not be so easily laid as she seemed to think. But, as the evenings grew longer and his plans for the installation of electric light began to materialize, he ceased to cast his eyes down those columns in *The Times*, *Country Life*, and other papers in which were painted, in glowing colours, the merits of family mansions and Elizabethan manor houses. By this time he had mentally argued away the uncanny impression left on his mind that night when he saw the screen slowly moving across the drawing-room, impelled by an unseen force. His healthy, buoyant scepticism returned to assure him that he had only *thought* he saw it move, and he began his old chaff again, with gusto.

But Peggy did not mind his chaff now. She was a match for him, having one weapon with which to lay him low—the word 'dumb-bells.' He could not argue against his own very decided action in the matter, and the word had thus a peculiar significance for him.

With the installation of the electric light came the cuckoo and nightingale, the thrushes, blackbirds, and the rest of the little feathered people, who sang all day and half the night over their broods in tree and hedge; the scented snow of fruit blossom haunted by myriad bees; the tears and laughter of green April. How the children loved being lifted in Daddy's arms to see the squirming, wide-mouthed babies in the nest, to be taken to the woods for primroses and watch the bunnies' twinkling tails disappear into the brown earth! The country was so lovely, the garden so lovably sweet that Peggy had to ask Joan Millis to come and revel with her; and Joan came.

Everything enchanted her, and she declared, over and over again, that she would not have known this place for the one she had visited in the autumn. She and Peggy talked till they were tired, about their children, and the laying of the ghost, a story that was capable of thrills. Joan overflowed with exultation in the fact that her old skinflint of a landlord had been, as she elegantly termed it, "dished."

"I never felt better pleased in my life," she asseverated. "He is such a selfish, greedy old pig that it serves him jolly well right. He has never done a ha-porth of good with his money in all his life. Your old man here must have been worth a dozen of his cousin."

They were sitting under the great beech tree, on a Sunday evening; the little fountain tinkling near and faint church bells chiming in the distance, to the accompaniment of bird melody all about them.

"Yes, he wasn't such a bad old boy," observed Percy: "and most of us are a bit cracked on one thing or another. We're cracked on our children, for instance. At least, Peg is. She can't see any faults in them, poor little blind looney!"

"The pot calls the kettle black," said Peggy, blandly. "Did you ever see anyone spoil children as Perks does, Joan? It is impossible for me to bring them up properly."

Joan laughed. There was a little pause, and she said:

"Well, you both seem reconciled to 'Hell Corner' now and I suppose there'll be no more talk of leaving it."

"We have another name for it," replied Percy. "We call it the Garden of Eden."

"Having banished the snake!"

"He objected to dumb-bells!" said Peggy, slyly.

"I wonder what Keary would say to that form of exorcism," Percy remarked, chuckling.

Joan smiled. "You've no idea," she said, "how it amuses me

to think that, after all Peggy's efforts, after Keary's disturbing visitation, letters to the Psychical Society, and so forth, it should have been good, prosaic, old Percy who did the trick and sent the wraith packing."

"I think of offering my services to the P. S. as an exorcist and spook-dispeller," he declared. "Do you think they'd take me on, Joan, at a decent salary?"

"I'm afraid you are too detrimental to furniture," she replied, laughing. "What do you think, Peg?"

"I think," said Peggy, "that, until Perks can logically explain why he smashed the screen, it would become him better to maintain a modest and discreet silence on the subject. And I would point out that if he had not been convinced there was some one behind the screen, the will would still be reposing there, and might be till we are all dust."

"You are right, O Fount of Wisdom," he agreed, "your crumpled slave grovels before you. Henceforth he will adopt a modest silence to cover his logical nakedness. But first I call you to witness, Joan, that I am an obvious 'medium' and the hiding-place of the missing will was revealed to me, rather than to my precious Tyrant."

"That is what makes it all so amusing," said Joan.

"The only thing that amuses me about it," said Peggy, "is the fact that Percy has had to climb down. He knows, as well as I do, that this house has been haunted and has no argument left to dispute it. If he were honest he would admit this."

Percy looked at Joan and his eyes twinkled.

"A wise man," he said, "never admits anything that may be used against him."

www.ingramcontent.com/pod-product-compliance
Lightning Source LLC
Chambersburg PA
CBHW020934310726
48980CB00007B/767/J

* 9 7 8 1 9 1 7 1 1 3 0 1 4 *